The room descended into a funeral hush
and Henry looked over to see, standing in the doorway, a most unexpected vision. He blinked. The countess?

How very young she looked. He had expected in the ten years since he last saw her for her to have grown into a grand dame, complete with whale bones, and past the first flush of youth.

Not this girl whose fingering of her fan appeared to contradict the confidence with which she held her frame; a girl who wore a simple cream colored Empire style dress and not, as far as he could discern, a touch of powder or other artifice. Even her chestnut brown hair was simply styled into the usual ringlets, held together with only pearl-tipped pins. He'd have expected an extraordinary coiffure piled impossibly high with a magnificent comb with a faux bird nestling on it.

And then she smiled and what otherwise might have truthfully been described as a rather plain countenance was transformed into a thing of beauty.

Not at all what he had expected of this evening, not the thing at all.

She looked directly at him and caught his eye. Henry stared, knew he stared. He didn't waver. The blue of her eyes dazzled him. Sapphire blue. He couldn't remember when he'd last noticed the color of a woman's eyes.

Henry unfurled his fingers that dug into his palms. Her simple beauty was an artifice in itself. Yes, he'd fallen for it. He'd been here before. He was only here to do what he had to do. He would not be so stupid as to fall for her again.

D0279853

Praise for *KRAKOW WALTZ*

"*KRAKOW WALTZ* is a deeply romantic and captivating story told against a rich and unusual background. The lead characters are very likeable, full of depth and substance. There is an intriguing plot, a wonderful atmosphere and some lovely touches of humor."

~Nicola Cornick, bestselling Regency romance author.

Krakow Waltz

by

Kate Allan

Krakow Waltz

Cover Art by *Tina Lynn*

The Wild Rose Press
PO Box 708
Adams Basin, NY 14410-0706
Visit us at www.thewildrosepress.com

Publishing History
First English Tea Rose Edition, 2010
Print ISBN 1-60154-805-2

Published in the United States of America

Dedication

For Ewa, John and Natalie

Miłość to cud, który zawsze może się znów zdarzyć.

Love is a wonder which can happen again.
Polish saying

Acknowledgments

Thank you to Verulam Writers' Circle and especially the contingent who used to meet at the late *Cafe Monsoon* in St Albans, and in particular Mary Woodward, Toby Frost, Ian Cundell and Jes Guy for your encouraging comments. Thank you also to Sue Child's thoughtful comments on an early draft. Thanks also to Justin for your help and encouragement.

Acknowledgments to Adam Mickiewicz, writer of *Pan Tadeusz* from which some of the Polish detail and humor have been borrowed, and Andrzej Wajda, who made the wonderful film version. Last but not least, to the city of Krakow and its beautiful buildings, streets and history, thank you for your inspiration, including the tragic memorial to Great Uncle Frederick, a Polish hussar, which may be found at the foot of the Wawel.

Prologue

Hampshire, England, 1791

Lord Wells stood on the lawn of his country estate. The square, red-brick house and orchards, sat nestled in the middle of a valley as though it had been stitched by a young lady onto her sampler.

As a member of the aristocracy, Wells sat occasionally in the Lords, but was infrequently in London. He preferred to take an interest in his farm and all the typical pursuits of a country gentleman. His abiding passion was hunting and he was known in the neighborhood for his kind nature and even temper. Two years ago he married a society beauty and brought her back to Hampshire to rusticate. Two years ago he believed he was one of the luckiest men alive.

He now believed he killed her by marrying her, for six months ago she died in childbed. The baby survived but Lord Wells could not bear to look at his daughter.

Indeed the torment was so strong she was banished to the nursery and he refused to enter those parts of the house where he might hear her crying and be reminded of her existence. He couldn't close his eyes without seeing the bloodied sheets he was not supposed to see, and hearing the cries of the newborn infant tearing through the air.

His grief was acute and time seemed to have worsened it.

That was why today he'd taken his favorite ivory-handled pistol from its rosewood box, primed it and strode across the lawns to the far reaches of the gardens.

The doctor had examined him several times. The servants whispered that he wasn't as he should be and it was unnatural to keep an infant shut away.

He raised the pistol and pulled the trigger.

Chapter One

London, 1807

Henry Edmund Champion found it easy to envelope himself in the idle conversation of a group of young bucks. All he had to do was hold a glass of champagne, sip it elegantly, feign that expression of perpetual ennui that fashion required and make a suitable lively crack now and again as the occasion demanded.

Yet Henry, only son of Mr. and Mrs. James Henry Champion of Sevenoaks, Kent, could not shake off his awareness that he shouldn't be here at all. It was only by the good graces of his old friend from school, Lord Brockleton, that he had secured an invitation to the Farringham's ball.

Henry pushed his shoulders back so his jacket sat squarer, tilted his chin slightly upwards and to one side and with an urbane expression swept his gaze over the room. Had it been a mistake to come?

Not when he saw her.

Barely ten feet away from him.

The usual hot stab at the sight of an attractive woman was completely expected. But not the rest: the stilling of every sinew in his body, pulled tight as over wound violin strings; the misting out of every other person in the room so that there was only her. The compulsion to believe that there had ever existed only one woman. That he never before had been so violently and wholly struck with desire.

Fustian! as his late aunt used to delight in saying. He noted attractive women all the time. Less frequently when he'd been on campaign, he admitted, but here in London, why they even dampened down their dresses to save gentlemen having to strain their imaginations too far.

Yet his gaze skimmed across her form, noting and calculating each inch and every angle. He followed the flare of her dress over her hips and to the floor, and then up, tracing the line of her décolletage; her neck, her oval face, the sweep of her dark eyelashes and the curve of her smile as she spoke to the dowager Lady Grantley.

And then, as if she knew, she caught his gaze. Her eyes widened, lips parted and brought a moment when ten feet between them disappeared. He might have been standing right next to her, able to reach out and touch her ebony curls. He might have smiled.

With a flick of her head she looked away.

He was still standing there, still holding his glass, still Henry Champion: the only person in the room not among the Upper Ten Thousand of high society.

She'd recognized him. Of course she had.

Or was he clinging onto some kind of effervescent hope that she remembered. That she had considered him more than simply a casual flirtation?

"Brockleton," Henry said. He could not help himself. "Who is that lady over there with the dark hair conversing with Lady Grantley? I believe I have met her before."

Brockleton spluttered. His eyes swiveled and bulged out of their sockets. He managed to swallow his mouthful of champagne. "That's the Honorable Miss Annabel Wells. Champion...." He lowered his voice to an urgent whisper. "Are you in jest?"

Like being thumped in the stomach with a dead weight, Henry's middle felt the sensation of being buckled. The look on Brockleton's face was not the thing at all. Even the smallest thing, a careless remark, a wrong glance, could be grist to the rumor mill.

"You're a good friend, Brockleton," Henry growled through a smile, "so for heaven's sake don't look at me like that. It might cause comment. I have no interest in the girl. Not in that way." *I'm not stupid enough to think I might be good enough for her,* he might well have said. A son of minor country gentry. Hardly eligible parti.

Brockleton wiped his brow with his sleeve and took a deep slug of his champagne.

Henry exhaled through his nose and cast what he intended to be an idle glance in her direction. "Ah, yes, I thought she looked familiar. I didn't recognize her if that is what you are wondering. We only met that one time. At your house party, I believe. I could easily be mistaken."

It was hardly an idle glance when the smallest glimpse of those dark ringlets pinned to the back of her head was enough to make him wince at the tightness of his breeches. And he had only met her once before, at Brockleton's, and only exchanged a short greeting with her and stayed by her side a few moments before some other gentleman had taken her away. But that had been enough to make a copperplate impression on his mind that could not be erased.

"She's pretty filly but a hoyden by all accounts." Brockleton dredged the last of his champagne. He raised his voice back to its ordinary hearty boom and looked around the company. "Right, I'm up for the card room. Who's joining me?"

A couple of fellows perked up. Henry followed them. He might as well squander a little money at cards. He had no heart for dancing. Not now.

Some hours later, when the air had grown

leaden with the heat of the bodies, the drink and the dancing and the first carriages had began to depart, Henry left the card room. He was up on the evening. Which was just as well. He couldn't afford to gamble. He looked about for Brockleton but couldn't see him anywhere. It appeared they were not to return to his house in Half Moon Street quite yet then.

Henry pulled himself up to the full height of his twenty-two years and took leave of the ballroom stuffed with heavy chatter and inharmonious laughter, to take a solitary amble on the terrace.

The fresh air, cold in his lungs, and quiet of the night revived him. He stood still and stared at the Chinese lanterns. Strung up in orderly lines, they cast a pleasing glow, lighting as far as the edge of the lawns.

All in all, he considered, nothing had happened. Nobody had cut him. For that at least he might be thankful. He'd survived some kind of test. A lady called Mrs. Franklin, who he understood to live close to Grosvenor Square, had said she would be sending him a card to a soiree. If he was to garner an invitation or two, and if Brockleton would put him up a while longer, he might as well stay in London for a time.

No one seemed about. Unusual perhaps because it was usually about now that unsuspecting debutantes were lured outside by undesirables intent on ruining reputations in return for making their fortunes via marriage.

The indistinct hum of conversations and music wafted out of the ballroom behind him. Where had Brockleton got to? He'd not seen him in the ballroom. Henry hoped he was not up to something he would later regret. He'd sworn blind the other day that he had no plans for marriage for two or three years yet.

"Unhand me, Freddy, or there'll be hell to pay!"

The shout came from somewhere in the darkness cracking across the lawns.

A lady's voice, clear as lead crystal, speaking defiantly but it was laced with fear. Henry closed his eyes, felt his chest heave. He didn't need this and he really hoped he was not going to find his friend in the middle of doing something very foolish.

How much had Brockleton had to drink?

Henry tapped down the stone steps and squashed the dew-wet lawn underfoot. He skidded. He regained his balance and pace quickly.

"Freddy! I said unhand me!"

He turned into the patch of darkness to the right, coming up against a tall hedge. There was no way through. He ran along the hedge until he found the gap. It was one of those gardens where the hedges were planted to form rooms. The moon was partially hidden by clouds and the light very faint but there was nothing in this room apart from a Grecian statue. The scuffling, breathing was somewhere farther on.

He darted through the gap to the right, towards the noise and into the next room and there was the man with a woman locked in his arms, forcing his kiss on her while she struggled to be free of him. Not Brockleton, thank heavens! Some other cad named Freddy.

"Hey!" Henry shouted. And immediately regretted it. He could do without drawing attention from the house. This was nothing to do with him, none of his business.

The man pulled off and the girl broke free.

Annabel Wells! With tears streaming down her eyes she flung herself two paces forward, landing desperately against him.

He must ignore his poor body, taut as iron, and place his reluctant arm around her quivering frame. To touch her was the thing he most, and least,

7

wanted to do.

The gentleman didn't wait to see if his honor would be challenged. Henry caught the flash of blind panic across his eyes, watched him stumble past them, breaking into a run. Just as well, really. He could do without the infamy of being involved in a duel with somebody.

"He's gone," Henry whispered to the shaking form planted in his arms. "Miss Wells," he said in the lowest voice he could. "Might I lend you my handkerchief?" He'd get her to dry her eyes and then he'd send her back to the ballroom, before somebody saw them, and... And...

She pulled her face away from where it had been buried in his jacket. "Oh, is that all you can do, lend me your... Oh!" She looked straight up at him. Her eyes widened. "Oh, no!"

She stepped clear of him and shifted her weight from one foot to the other and held her arms folded in front of her. Her dress was rather thin, silk and she wore nothing else against the cold. She shivered and he could see the bumps of gooseflesh on her arms and across her collar-bone. "Oh, dear, Mr. Champion, you have interrupted my carefully laid scheme!" she said.

Henry drew a sharp breath. She remembered his name! "What plan?" he heard himself say.

She caught his gaze, held it with her dark eyes that sparkled with tears, reflecting the silvery moonlight. He knew he was lost.

"Isn't it obvious?" Her voice was laced with scorn yet she sniffed back a tear. "I had lured Freddy Hepplethwaite out here. You see he has had a *tendre* for me for such a long time and he nearly offered for me, but then, his mama..." She sniffed. "You may as well know as someone will be bound to tell you sooner or later. My reputation is in tatters. They say I am a hoyden because I cantered unchaperoned across Hyde Park with... A gentleman followed me, a notorious rake. Certain...gossips...saw. The only way I can salvage myself is by marriage so I have to catch a husband. I had hoped to force Freddy into making a declaration. We've known each other since childhood. I always thought... And now... " She hid her face in her hands as tears wracked her body.

"I..." He couldn't say it.

And there was something else he couldn't quite put his finger on. There was something incredible about how her manner should be as attractive to him as her form. The way she had thought on her feet, her perception of her problem and the solution she had proposed to it.

"I have to marry. Someone very honorable so no one will dare say a thing," she went on to explain as she blinked back her tears.

Henry started to pull at his jacket. Her flimsy silk dress was not suited to a chilly April evening. "Are you not cold? Shall we go back indoors?"

"And what, exactly, do we have here?" A deep female voice cut through the darkness.

Too late.

Henry cleared his throat. "Madam, you have erroneously perceived the situation."

"Oh, have I? And how is that, pray tell?"

He'd been about to say that he was here because he had interrupted another fellow but that would only make things worse for the Honorable Miss Wells.

"Explain yourself, young sir!" the matron demanded.

"Quite right," came the voice of a second lady.

He turned to appraise them. Just as he suspected. Both with their beady eyes and cruel smiles. And nothing better to do than indulge in *on-dits* and dash people's reputations against rocks of their making.

Miss Wells pulled away from him, slowly and with not an inch of guilt or shame on her face. "Put your cat claws away, Mrs. Dorcester, or the Ton might be interested to hear…"

"Yes, yes," said the lady who must be Mrs. Dorcester, "but when will they hear it? When you are outside of Society you will not have its ear, m'dear."

"I am to be married but I am not about to tell you about it." Her voice held not an ounce of hesitation. Her tone rang out as clear as a bell. It tapped the final nail in the coffin of his hope. Hope? How stupid he was. Henry wanted to kick himself. He never had any right to have any hope with regards to Miss Wells.

"You expect me to believe that?" Mrs. Dorcester cried.

Henry took a step forward. And then faltered. What could he say? Especially as Miss Wells had unknowingly wounded him in the middle of his chest. So much so that it hurt. He had no right to be surprised. No right to object.

He wanted to walk away.

The second lady came forward. She seized Miss Wells's silk-gloved hands and kissed them. "My dear, what superior news!"

Another lady appeared out of the blackness to congratulate her, and then another, a peacock feather bouncing ridiculously from the top of her turban.

Henry knew the smile he had contrived was false. He didn't even know who these people were. And now they started to come thick and fast. Like moths to a flame.

"Miss Wells looks as though she could do with a moment to compose herself," said an elderly lady, her wizened neck arrayed with splendid diamonds. She tapped her ivory fan on her wrist. "My dear, come back with me to the ballroom."

"Yes, aunt," replied Miss Wells, her expression uncharacteristically meek. She accompanied her aunt back towards the house.

The well-wishers melted away. Henry found himself alone, standing on the enclosed piece of lawn with high hedges all around him and in half-darkness. He put his head in his hands and groaned, felt his knees buckle and sank to the ground. The grass was wet and cold. He didn't care.

He'd thought about getting married in some minor compartment in his mind. He'd thought he'd come to consider it a few years hence. Or however many years it took before he came into his meager inheritance. As he stood now he could not afford to marry.

He should never even have looked at her!

That was impossible, but he should not have allowed himself to dream. Yet meeting her was like putting freshly roasted beef in front of a man who had not eaten for three days.

The back of his neck prickled. Henry had the sense he was being watched. He scrambled to his feet and made a futile attempt to rub the damp from the knees of his breeches. Sure enough a couple of ladies had thought to stop awhile and regard him.

He stared at them and they broke into a fast and fan-fluttering chatter and moved rapidly away, out of the garden.

Alone with only the moon and stars to witness, something akin to anger rose inside him. Then a sense of weariness overwhelmed him. He had not the luxury of idleness these people enjoyed, their lives revolving around balls and hunting, and house parties. He had come to London because his old headmaster recommended him to some fellow and tomorrow he had an appointment at the Home Office. Staying with Brockleton was a convenience and saved him the cost of lodgings.

He should not have come here tonight. Henry breathed deeply and walked, his chin held high, back towards the ballroom. He should not have allowed himself to make decisions on a whim. Calf-love, they called it. He would not make such a mistake again.

****

Annabel kept her arm firmly entwined in her aunt's as if her life depended on it. She would go back into the ballroom as if nothing had happened. She would not look back. Not even allow herself to consider the possibility. That man, Mr. Champion, or whatever he was improbably called, was nothing to her. Nor could he ever be. A member of the minor gentry, with no fortune to his name. What such a man was doing at a grand affair like this, she did not know.

"There is a distinct chill," her aunt remarked. "For April."

Annabel thrust her chin in the air and muttered an inconsequential reply. He must have connections, Mr. Champion, but they counted for nothing without pedigree and property. She had vowed to catch a husband with both. She needed to. Her father's debts—his suicide—meant her own portion would be very modest. If indeed there was anything left. She was only here because of the kindness and charity of her aunt and godmother, Lady Roseley.

What choice did she have?

Annabel blinked back a pair of tears. She'd thought she could rely on Freddy, she just had to provide the opportunity but he'd bolted. He had let her down badly and now who else was there...? She would not think about that now. It threatened to provoke emotions that were inconvenient to the present moment. She ought to have only one thing on her mind at present, that of how to ensure she was married as quickly as possible.

"Lady Roseley. Miss Wells." Lady Belham, a tall widow whom Annabel had never liked, greeted them as they entered the ballroom. "Taking the air, I see?" Her beady eyes gleamed with intent. "Might I introduce Count Piotr Szalynski?"

"Lady Roseley," the count said, his voice crisp and clear, yet unmistakably foreign. "Your servant." He stepped forward and gave a bow to her aunt before turning to her. "Miss Wells. Your servant."

"Count Szalynski." She nodded. Of course, they had met. They had danced only yesterday.

"Count, how delightful to see you again," her aunt said allowing him to kiss her gloved hand. "I see you know my niece already. How wonderful."

"We have met on two occasions I believe, Lady Roseley. How could I forget?"

Annabel lifted her gaze to see that he was looking at her closely. A sudden hope rose within her that he would ask her to dance again. Then, she might speak with him, flirt with him a little, and maybe... Annabel smiled. He was a handsome man; impeccably attired, tall and athletic-looking. His complexion was swarthy and Annabel supposed that he spent a lot of time outdoors. It made a change from the pale-faced young English gentlemen she was used to, their cheeks oft flushed with a combination of drink and the heat of the thousand wax candles that lit every ballroom.

"Something amuses you, Miss Wells?" he said.

"I expect it is the champagne," Annabel replied and opened her fan. Many considered champagne unsuitable for young ladies but Annabel found it erased some of her shyness, made it easy to be flirtatious. She added, to ensure he would not think badly of her, "I am not used to it."

"Your fan might produce a mild effect, but a better remedy could be to take some exercise, to

13

dance." He offered his hand. He was so gallant. She liked that. "Miss Wells?"

Annabel accepted with a small nod of her head. He would be terribly rich, she was sure, seignior of thousands and thousands of acres. As for his bloodline, she would probably discover he was related to royalty.

The champagne had given her the idea that she could parson's mousetrap Freddy Hepplethwaite. Perhaps the failure of her scheme would prove a blessing after all. Could she engineer a proposal from Count Szalynski?

After tonight, her declaration of an impending marriage, she desperately needed a suitable future husband.

"My estates are in the Austrian part of Poland," he told her as they danced. "I am only in London for a short time."

"Oh." Annabel gave a suitably downcast expression. "But..." She shook her head. "Forgive me, I should not be so forward as to presume an acquaintance."

His reply was a smile. "But we are acquainted. You forget, I know your aunt and uncle. Before I return to Paris, if it is allowed, I shall call on you. Might you be at home tomorrow?"

"I do not believe we are visiting tomorrow," Annabel replied. She would make certain of it. She was determined to be Countess Szalynski. "Berkeley Square."

Chapter Two

Nine years later

Henry became aware that he was face down on the ground, that his right cheek laid on hard pavement and that various parts of his body ached. He had no inclination to open his eyes. Cold chaffed at his wrists and the back of his head, which must therefore be hatless. He could hear horses' hooves, the clatter of wheels, the rattle of vehicles. His head hurt. Was he lying in the street?

"The devil take it, Champion!" came a loud exclamation, painfully close to his ear. The voice was familiar but he couldn't attach a name or a face to it. "I'd recognize those blond tresses anywhere! Dear, oh, dear. Where's your man, eh?"

Man? The voice must mean his former valet, Robards.

"Had to let him go," Henry heard himself reply. He hiccupped. "Dun territory."

"You might well be in dun territory but you're also in a public street. Come on, let's get you up and on your feet and somewhere a little more comfortable, eh?"

It was a tricky maneuver. Somehow, in the middle of manhandling him up from the pavement, his companion must have managed to call a hansom. Henry found himself inside a cab, propped up by the squabs and face-to-face with his old friend, Jonathan Harvey.

"Harvey! Not seen you since that time in Lisbon."

"Lisbon?" Jonathan smiled. "You've forgotten that we met two weeks ago in a certain gaming hell in Covent Garden."

Henry tried to recall. He had an idea of the club but the rest was fog.

"Now, where are we going?" Jonathan leaned forward. "Have you lodgings?"

"Yes, but not here. Cheapside." The unfashionable end of town. He gave the address. Jonathan leaned out of the coach and instructed the driver. He slammed the door shut. They moved off with a jolt. Henry felt sick.

"Hard times, eh?"

Henry did not reply. It came back into his memory piece by piece and he wasn't sure if he wanted to remember it.

"I heard you did rather well in the war?"

"Yes." That much was true. A minor hero of Waterloo, he'd been feted like the best of them when he'd first returned to London. Yet he could have met a French bullet as easily as Brockleton had. "But..." He wasn't sure what to say.

"Fickle times." Jonathan leaned back and drew a snuff box from a top pocket. He flicked its enamel lid open and held it out towards Henry.

"Never could stand the stuff," Henry replied.

"You've not lost all your senses then. Filthy habit." Jonathan snapped the snuff box shut and replaced it in his pocket.

Henry cast his gaze out of the window and at the passing street. Drab, the shops and tenements looked. Not a good part of town.

"You're too fine a fellow to be sacrificed to the whimsy of lady luck. Eh, Champion? You listening?"

Henry looked back at his friend. Jonathan wore a serious expression.

"So you had to let Robards go? Know where he might be found?"

"He's probably at my lodgings." Henry sighed. "Stubborn he is. Loyal, too. Says he won't go until the last penny is gone. Well, it's packed its bags and gone."

"Capital! Sensible fellow, Robards. I'll square things up with him, and then we'll see about finding you something to do."

"I don't think you understand. It's all gone. The house. Everything."

"You're not the first person to squander away their inheritance. You think your friends want to see you in the gutter?"

"There's plenty who deserve charity. Widows. Orphans." Henry ached all over. His head pounded. He wanted to lie down. "Not me. I've been an utter fool."

****

If Henry had been asked to wager that day that less than a se-night later he would be an invited guest at a musical evening given by an important Society hostess, he'd have declined the wager. Only yesterday he had attended a summons to the Home Office. Shortly, he was to depart for the Vienna Congress as an aide to Wellington. It was not a military commission, but his expenses would be paid. In the meantime, secure in a small yet befittingly gentlemanly set of rooms in St James's, the invitation cards had begun to arrive. Jonathan Harvey had been as good as his word.

Henry tilted his chin an inch higher. He could see over the shoulders of the audience to the mirrors hung on the back wall of the long salon. They reflected the sturdy rear view of the velvet-clad Italian opera singer, her ridiculously high-pinned hair, the quintet of seated musicians, their elbows flying. Also reflected were the politely bored faces of the overheating audience, seated and at the back, like him, standing. As one of the seated ladies shifted her rapidly moving fan a few inches to the side, he saw his own reflection in one of the long, heavily gilded mirrors. Henry Champion, aide to the Duke of Wellington and to His Britannic Majesty's government. He liked that. That his countenance was illuminated by the candlelight to look rather yellow, making his complexion a similar shade to his blond hair, he liked a little less. Yet he was impeccably turned out by Robards, his cravat perfectly tied—

A hand tapped his shoulder.

Henry turned.

He was surprised to see Jonathan Harvey. He shifted aside to allow him to have a better view.

The opera singer pushed relentlessly towards the pinnacle of her aria. Henry shut his eyes. He didn't need to see, it was awful enough simply listening.

He felt the tap on his shoulder again and Henry turned to see he was being beckoned to step outside. He followed Jonathan into the hall and shut the door behind them.

Jonathan coughed. It echoed through the empty corridor. "I have some news for you." He spoke in a low voice. "It couldn't wait."

"I am obliged to you. Opera has never been my thing."

"You might only be needed in Vienna a few weeks, is that not true?" Jonathan raised his eyebrows. "So I thought, why go all that way and then come back again. I took the liberty of writing to an old friend of mine. You know him too. His reply arrived this afternoon."

"Who? You're talking in riddles."

"Wait!" Jonathan held up his hand. "That is not all. My father came to hear about what is a rather... delicate situation. And suddenly it all came together in my mind that you would be the perfect person.

18

Not least because you will be in Vienna anyway."

"You are still talking in riddles."

"And there is, from what I understand, a substantial sum of money available. Enough to buy back your inheritance at least. My father will explain to them that you are a gentleman, but one in very reduced circumstances."

"Jonathan, I trust you completely as a friend, but I still have no idea what you are talking about."

"You remember Count Ralenski?"

"Yes, I do." Henry smiled. He'd liked the count from when they had first met. "We met in Paris in 1814 and again in Brussels after Waterloo. He was a captain in a Hussar regiment—"

"Yes," Jonathan said. "He remembers you well, and would be delighted to meet you in Vienna and, when your business there is concluded, have you as his guest in Poland."

"How wonderful for me. And what is the real purpose of this holiday?"

Jonathan fingered his clean-shaven chin. "It is a delicate matter as I mentioned. A family matter. The utmost discretion is required. They are an elderly couple and they would like to meet you themselves. My father has spoken to them about you and they would like to see you at your earliest convenience." Jonathan gave the address.

Berkeley Square. One of the most fashionable addresses in London.

****

"Lieutenant Champion?" The elderly Lady Roseley rose from her chaise-longue and offered her hand. Henry appraised her briefly: her modish costume in peacock blue, her expertly-dressed hair, the contours of her countenance. High cheekbones and a high forehead. A beauty in her own day, he expected.

"Mr. Champion, ma'am." He bowed and kissed

her hand. "Your servant. I have cashed out of the Army."

Confusion crossed her powdered face. "From what I understand, Mr. Champion, you are to accompany Wellington to Vienna? For the peace negotiations?"

"Indeed I am, ma'am. I leave next week."

"Will you take tea?" she said, her voice lighter.

"Yes, thank you," he said.

She issued the instruction to the footman who had showed him into the drawing room. There was a gentleness about her. He found himself warming to her.

"Do sit down." She sat down herself. "Lord Roseley is expected home shortly. If you would be so good as to wait until he returns?"

"If you can bear my company for tea, ma'am, it would be my pleasure." He chose a comfortable looking chair opposite her.

"And a pleasant diversion for me also," she replied. "Will you tell me a little of yourself. Were you at Waterloo?"

"Yes, ma'am." He pressed his lips together. It must be that Lady Roseley did not go out into Society that much, for surely she would have heard him feted as *Lieutenant Champion, minor hero of Waterloo*. Nothing to compare to the great hero of course, but someone who had been there, and whose small part had, apparently, *mattered*—

"Mr. Champion?" Lady Roseley's quiet voice brought him out of his reverie. "I am sorry if my question stirred up memories you would rather were forgotten."

"No, no," he assured her. "It is only that I have been asked to give my account of Waterloo so many times now, I fear I have lost a little interest in the telling of it." He smiled. He might as well talk of it again. She would want to hear as much about the

Duchess of Richmond's ball as what happened on the fateful day itself. "I shall endeavor to give my best account."

"Splendid." Lady Roseley relaxed back into her chaise.

He'd told her most of it before a tall man, past sixty, with ruddy cheeks came into the room, unannounced nor accompanied by any servant. Lord Roseley.

"My lord," his wife said. She nodded her head but did not rise. "Lieut—Mr. Champion is here."

Henry stood up and shook Roseley's hand. Roseley did not go so far as to smile but there was a jolliness about his expression. He had more vigor than his wife and sat down heavily, crossing his legs and pulling a pouch from his pocket. He took a generous pinch of snuff before speaking.

"Champion? In London long?"

"A few more days," Henry replied and wondered where this all was leading.

"I am given to understand that you are a man of impeccable character. What do you say to that?"

"That you have been speaking to my friends, my lord."

Roseley gave a laugh that provoked a chesty cough.

"My lord," Henry said. "If I might be of any assistance to you I shall."

"Can we trust him, my dear?" Roseley turned and looked at his wife.

"We have spoken at some length before you came home," she replied. "Mr. Champion is courteous, kind, and I would venture to presume, honorable."

"I fear the truth is that we have little choice in the matter." Roseley turned back to face Henry. "My wife cannot possibly travel to the Continent, and I cannot leave her."

21

"You wish me to act on your behalf in...Vienna?"

"Not Vienna. Krakow. I understand that you had accepted an invitation to visit that city in the spring?"

"Yes, my lord."

Lord Roseley looked about his fine, well proportioned drawing room seemingly in thought. He rose to his feet and pulled the damask-corded bell.

"Brandy," he said. He waved at the tantalus on the sideboard. "Not that stuff. I want the good stuff from the cellar."

A servant appeared, to whom he gave very precise instructions.

"Krakow is the ancient Polish capital where her kings were buried." Lord Roseley paced up to the top fringes of the vast oriental rug that carpeted the room and stood, his back framed by a tall set of French windows, hands clasped behind his back. "Krakow's market square is the largest in Europe. There, twenty years ago, the national hero, Tadeusz Kosciuszko, first rallied the standard and mustered men demanding the return of Poland to Polish hands. It is exactly the place where the cause of Polish nationalism might be allowed to develop unhindered by authority that might threaten the newly won peace. It seems to me that if the balance of power in Europe is to be disturbed it is in such a place that it could happen."

"Yes, my lord," Henry said as Roseley paused.

"But that is somewhat by the by. I am not a politician or a general." Roseley waved his hand in the same manner as he had done towards the tantalus. "This concerns my niece, who is in Krakow. We want her home in England. We believe that she may be in some difficulty in Krakow. Not in any immediate danger but there was some unpleasantness over some of her late husband's lands. Her husband's brother will sort the matter out but he remains in Russia at present. He is tied to the court of Tsar Alexander. When he returns to Poland, however, there will be no reason for our niece to stay in Krakow. We would like you to bring her home to England with you when you return."

The minor hero of Waterloo was being asked to be a rescuer of maidens? Henry was unsure what to say. Of course, there was no reason why any gentleman should not offer to accompany the Roseley's niece back to England. Notwithstanding that Jonathan had mentioned money. If there was a small profit to be made in addition to his travel being funded, really he was in no position to refuse.

"My lord," Henry said, "it would be my honor to serve you."

Lord Roseley's taut features relaxed. "Capital! Now where the devil is our brandy?"

"I shall write to our niece and tell her to expect you when, Mr. Champion?" Lady Roseley's eyes shone bright.

"I am afraid it will be unlikely to be much before the new year. The peace negotiations are not expected to conclude for some weeks."

"I will give you, of course, her direction. She is the Countess Szalynski, though we think of her still as our Annabel."

Henry's throat tightened. "Annabel...Annabel Wells?"

"Yes, as she was before her marriage to the count." Lady Roseley smiled. "Were you acquainted?"

Annabel Wells. A name he had not heard spoken in years. Nine years. Henry brought his attention back to Lord Roseley who was still talking.

"It goes without saying that we will bear all the expenses of your journey."

Annabel Wells. She would not look as she did nine years ago, he was sure. She would have thickened from childbearing and she would wear matronly dresses in gaudy colors. Not delicate silks that seemed to blend with her skin.

"The marriage produced no children," Lord Roseley said, startling Henry with the notion that his mind was being read.

A flicker of sadness seemed to pass behind Roseley's eyes. "It is only Annabel to bring back to England."

Nine years ago, he'd vowed to forget her. Yet, it could not matter now, not after so much time.
****

Annabel woke at the sound of squeaking. Was it mice? Or rats? She shuddered and pulled the heavy bedcovers up to her chin. She had been dreaming. Dreaming back to a long time ago, when she had made her debut in London Society. She turned over. It was an English bed, constructed of oak, sturdily-made and with a well-sprung mattress. It had come here to Krakow a generation before she had.

Nine years ago, now she thought back on it.

Was it really only nine years? It seemed like a lifetime. Yet her aunt's letter had brought it back in all its freshness.

She pulled herself up to reach the jug of water on the small table beside the bed. Cold air tickled her shoulders and it reminded her of the cold night air of the Farringham's garden. The evening that changed everything, sealed the direction of her life. Oh, the folly of youth! She had given her shallow feelings more due than they were worth.

She poured a glass quickly and drank. Ice-cold it stung her throat and made her gasp. Half full, she left the glass on the table and curled back up in bed.

The grayness of the room sat still around her so that she could only see the far drapes of the bed as if they were suspended in a mist.

If only that ridiculous incident had never

happened in the gardens at the Farringham's ball. She had been utterly stupid to think that she could catch a husband by luring Freddy Hepplethwaite into the gardens so that they might be caught in a compromising situation and Freddy would be forced to declare himself.

She turned her feather pillow over and punched it to plump it up. She sank her head into its revived softness. What had even given her the idea that Freddy might make a suitable husband? She could not remember now. She would have been better off marrying that very ordinary fellow, Mr. Champion. Strangely, she had never forgotten him. Not even through these long years. There was something about him that had sent her pulse racing in a way that defied explanation. He was not a man of property or title. Not eligible at all.

Would that happen when she met him again? Would her spine tingle, a tingle that traveled all the way down to her toes? Would her mind empty of all cognitive thought, dazed as it were by the mere presence of him? Would her breath become heavy and difficult to muster?

Or would he be barely recognizable, a man firmly into middle age? He almost certainly had a wife and children.

She closed her eyes. The misty darkness hung around in her mind's eye. From it emerged the precise, delicate handwriting of her aunt on letter paper:

Mr. Champion is to come to Krakow, he supposes in the Spring. He would be delighted to escort you back to England when he returns himself. I so look forward to seeing you again, my dear niece...;

And;

Mr. Champion was decorated at Waterloo. Indeed he has a reputation as somewhat of a minor hero of that great event, and of course he travels to be a trusted aide to Wellington at Vienna. Roseley and I had no hesitation as to his character and therefore you will be entirely safe in his protection.

Annabel felt a tear moving slowly down her cheek. She punched the pillow again but its softness brought no comfort. She had brought the way things had turned out on herself.

Chapter Three

Seven months later

Henry pulled the lapels of his evening coat so it sat straighter on his shoulders and left the dressing room. He skimmed the smooth banister with his gloved hand and hastened down two flights of wide, curving stairs. Count Marek Ralenski's residence was a grand five-storey townhouse built during the Renaissance in the Italian style and situated in the heart of the city of Krakow.

Ralenski was waiting in the hall. He wore his Hussar's dress uniform and looked immaculate from his shining boots up to his magnificent shako which he held under one arm. An inch or so taller than Henry he was as lanky as a whippet and sported a wispy, jet-black moustache. His splendor made up a little for the fact that his dark hair had started to thin and that his deep set features made him look rather stern when he forgot to smile.

Beau Brummel had a lot to answer for, Henry mused. In contrast to Marek, he was dressed plainly in black, cream and drab. The almost-obligatory sartorial uniform of London, here made him feel like a parson. In Poland the ladies dressed in Empire fashions from Paris, but the gentlemen held on to their colorful uniforms from the past and some even went out with furs draped over their shoulders as if they had just come back from the hunt.

When Marek mentioned last night that they had been invited to dine this evening with Countess Szalynski, he was surprised. Not least because they had only arrived in Krakow the day before yesterday. News travelled fast, Marek assured him, and the countess was a great hostess with whom he often dined. He had been great friends with her late husband. Henry speculated on whether and how the countess had come to hear of his arrival in Krakow, for he'd not yet written to her, but at least he was saved the trouble of effecting an introduction.

"You appear in a reverie, my friend?" Marek raised a thin eyebrow. "Shall we go?"

"Yes, I'm ready," Henry replied. As ready as he'd ever be. What did it matter whether the countess knew of his arrival yet or not?

"You will enjoy meeting the countess, Henry. Not only because she is English." Marek winked.

Henry took a deep breath. It mattered because he felt slightly sick in his stomach and wore such plain clothes he felt as though he had nowhere to hide. If he was truthful with himself, he was nervous. How foolish to be nervous of meeting a lady he'd not set eyes on for nine...no, ten years!

"Did the countess specifically invite me to join you?"

"Henry, stop being pedantic. How could the countess know of your visit here? Where I dine, you dine. You will be a great surprise to her. She will be delighted to meet you. There are not many English in Krakow."

"Yes..." Henry caught Marek's eye. He regarded him curiously.

"Henry! Even a staid and sober fellow like yourself won't be immune. You'll see."

"Perhaps." Henry shrugged his shoulders and hoped Marek would change the subject. He didn't want to talk about his finer feelings. Not now, not even in jest.

"Ah!" Marek frowned. "Don't let one woman's wiles cloud you to appreciating the female form."

Henry could have done without the reminder. He busied himself putting on his cape held out by the footman.

"You think too deeply, my friend," Marek continued. "When you get back to England you will easily find a sweet little thing who will be only too happy to marry a dashing war hero. In the meantime..." Marek took his scarf from a footman and wound it around his neck. "Even Bonaparte had the sense to take a Polish mistress. They are more faithful, as a rule."

That cut to the quick. Henry pressed his lips together, willed himself not to react. Marek had known how thoroughly he'd been humiliated by a certain woman. All of Vienna knew it.

"We'll walk, it's only the next street. Oh, damn." Marek patted distractedly at his pockets. Then he said something in Polish and the footman started before Marek stilled him.

"I've forgotten my snuff box," Marek said to Henry, grinning. "I'll go and get it myself. Will be quicker than waiting for a servant. I know exactly where I left it."

"Shall I go on ahead?" He could do with some fresh air. The thought that he was shortly to meet Annabel Wells again disturbed him more than he had expected. She would be older now, much less attractive, he repeated to himself. He would probably not even recognize her.

"I won't be a minute," Marek said. "Just turn right out of the house and then take the first street on the left."

Marek bounded upstairs and Henry let the footman open the front door for him and stepped down into the paved street, *Ulica Florianska*, or in English *Florianska Street*, and turned right as instructed.

It was cold for an April night. Not that he was

any sort of expert on the continental climate. *Ulica Florianska* was a wide thoroughfare; not a boulevard or avenue, Krakow's streets were medieval, but wide enough for two carriages to pass each other easily. During the day there had been regular traffic. Now the street was quiet and empty.

The first street on the left was little more than an alleyway, and in the dusk, very dark. Ten paces down it Henry stopped. He'd better wait for Marek, and back on *Ulica Florianska*. He might have taken the wrong street.

Henry heard footsteps behind him. He turned.

Two men stood facing him, blocking his path.

"What the devil?" Henry slid two fingers down between his cravat and his neck and tugged it looser.

Where they footpads? A burley man and his lankier partner acted careful to keep their faces hidden by the shadows. Their arms dangled at their sides, shoulders half hunched at the ready...to pounce?

He heard his heart thumping against his chest. If he went for the lankier one first and got him out of the way then that would be his best chance. Where they armed? He couldn't see—

Someone shouted, utterly incomprehensible. Threatening enough that the two men immediately turned on their heels and fled.

The even clatter of a single pair of heavy boots was coming up behind him.

Henry swung around. A tall man emerged from the shadows. Henry caught a glint, the blade of the man's drawn sword reflecting the moonlight. His breath stilled.

As the man came closer Henry saw the shining flecks of the silver buckled splendor of a dress uniform. A noble—Henry's spirits rose.

The noble shouted something in Polish with a voice like a thunderous boom.

"Good evening," Henry replied in French and ventured a smile and then hesitated. He should have tried English or German instead. So far being English had universally resulted in being welcomed with open arms but...

"Ah, ha! English, no?" A bellow of a laugh erupted from the stranger. His pearl white teeth glistened like his sword. Then he sheaved his sword. That was certainly a good sign. "You must be Ralenski's friend, for there is only one Englishman I have heard about in town?"

"Yes, I am Count Ralenski's English guest." Henry extended his hand but the noble gave him a crushing embrace and slapped him heartily on the back.

"I'm Count Zakonski, Piotr. That's Peter in English. Like Saint Peter." He laughed again. It echoed through the narrow confines of the alleyway.

"Mr. Henry Champion." Henry straightened himself upright again, resisted the temptation to pull his coat back into shape lest the count took offence. He hadn't yet warmed to his new acquaintance.

"Now you shouldn't be hanging around at night like this, Mr. Champagne—"

"Champion," Henry corrected.

"Champion, ah!" The count raised his hands into the air, smiled as if they were sharing the greatest of jokes.

"Henry?" The clipped shout came from behind. Henry turned to see Marek striding up the alley toward them. About time! He breathed a long, steady breath.

"Ralenski!" Zakonski greeted Marek by seizing his entire arm.

"Count Zakonski, good evening," Marek replied before pulling away and straightening his cloak in his usual devil-may-care manner. "Henry, where did you get to? You only stepped outside and when I came down into the street I couldn't see you anywhere."

"Some of these little streets," Zakonski said, leaning forward and shaking his head. "Not safe. Stick to the main streets, eh?"

Henry wondered what Zakonski was doing down this tiny street. Not that he wasn't thankful for his intervention. It had been a near run thing anyway. He would have said the odds were even of him being able to fight the footpads off by himself.

"Let's go," Marek said waving an arm. "Zakonski, I take it you're going to the Countess Szalynski's?"

"Of course." Zakonski swung around, bearing his teeth in the full force of a grin, and his green cloak swished majestically. "I am on my way there."

Zakonski's expression could only be described as arrogant and, sartorially, he had an old European feel to him, with the fur draped across his shoulders.

Marek led the way and Henry kept at his heels, conscious that their new friend was only a pace behind them. Within a hundred yards they had emerged onto *Ulica Szpitalna,* or *Hospital Street,* and they walked up the street heading towards the city walls. They passed only a few houses before Marek stopped outside a large house on their left, freshly distempered. Although the four-storied residence was undoubtedly as old as its neighbors it looked as new as a brand new pin. The stonework must have been recently cleaned as well.

"The countess has a cellar as you say, no?" Zakonski raised a bushy eyebrow. Marek lifted his hand to pull the iron rod of the bell.

"Yes," Marek said, "a fine cellar." He clicked his heels and stood up straight giving Henry the impression his manner towards Zakonski was unusually formal. Henry wondered why. They were both Poles and they certainly appeared to be acquainted with one another.

A small door cut into one of the vast wooden double doors opened and a male servant in a smart livery and etched countenance ushered them in. If the servant was anything to go by then the countess was socially of the first water.

They were shown through the wide stone flagged hallway and up the curving stairs, and into a salon on the first floor.

Henry fastened his hands tightly behind his back.

The heat from the large stove in the countess's salon seemed as burning as the crackling tension in the room such that even a stranger to this city could not fail to notice it. Gathered in what was otherwise a very typical salon with its fine paintings, gilt mirrors and fabulous wallpapers were above a dozen men. All men, Henry noted with interest. Where were their wives?

So many candles, the smell of beeswax was quite distinct, and the way they glittered as each flame was reflected repeatedly in the many mirrors gave the room a stately aura. It was only a room in a moderate townhouse but it could have been a palace. What kind of woman—

Marek clicked his tongue. "This is a political dinner," he whispered in Henry's ear. "You had better turn your attentions to the countess, my friend, for you'll be sorely pressed for any entertainment from these bores."

Henry smiled. They might have fought on different sides but now he was proud to number Marek as one of his friends and his wry sense of humor so often hit the mark.

"Come," Zakonski said with an imperious gesture, "let me introduce you to some of our city's friends." He coughed as if to muffle his remaining words. "And some of her enemies."

Why had he said that? Henry felt the hackles on the back of his neck rise.

They went forward and Henry was immediately introduced to two Russians, in French. Henry was thankful. He could keep up a sophisticated conversation in French. Yet he could not relax. Where was she? Did she let all her guests gather first before joining them? Would they not see her until they were called to dinner?

The room descended into a funeral hush and Henry looked over to see, standing in the doorway, a most unexpected vision. He blinked. The countess?

How very young she looked. He had expected in the ten years since he'd seen her last that she would have grown into a grande dame, complete with whale bones, and well past her first flush of youth.

Not this girl whose fingering of her fan appeared to contradict the confidence with which she held her frame; a girl who wore a simple cream colored Empire-style dress and not, as far as he could discern, a touch of powder or other artifice. Even her chestnut brown hair was simply styled into the usual ringlets, held together only with pearl-tipped pins. He'd have expected an extraordinary coiffure piled impossibly high with a magnificent comb with a faux bird nestling on it or some such fancy.

And her jewelry was equally understated. An elegant three stringed pearl necklace and... He searched for more in vain.

And then she smiled and what might have otherwise truthfully been described as a rather plain countenance was transformed into a thing of beauty.

Not at all what he'd expected of this evening, not the thing at all.

She looked directly at him, caught his eye. Henry stared, knew that he stared. He didn't waver. The blue of her eyes were dazzling. Sapphire blue.

He couldn't remember when he had last noticed the color of a woman's eyes. She lifted her eyebrows fractionally and seemed to appraise him before turning her head ever so slightly and dropping his gaze.

Henry coughed, put his fist to his mouth. Across the room they all smiled at her in return. He could have smiled, couldn't he? No doubt he'd looked to her like a gaping fish.

The truth was he'd been stunned just for that moment, hadn't expected her to single him out at first glance and stare at him like that.

Well, let them all smile at her if they wanted. Henry swallowed something that had risen in his throat that resembled annoyance.

He could see it now. Her simple beauty was an artifice in itself. Designed no doubt to distract, throw every man in the room off his balance because she made it so damned easy to imagine undressing her. A flimsy gown, a necklace and some hairpins were all that needed removing.

Henry unfurled his fingers that were digging into his palms. Yes, he'd fallen for it. He'd been here before. He was here only to do what he had to do. He would not be so stupid as to fall for her again.

The countess turned to the man on her right, a gentleman with a roguish smile to which Henry had not been previously introduced.

"That's Hantenberg, Austrian, a devil." Henry felt a slight tug on his sleeve and he turned his head to see Marek's face a hair's breadth from his own.

Henry nodded as imperceptibly as he could and Marek drifted away. He repeated the name in his mind so he didn't forget it. Hantenberg. He impressed the small man's sharp features on his memory so he would recognize him again. It was interesting that an Austrian should be here. They'd not been happy that Krakow had been granted free

35

city status, when it otherwise would have been part of Galicia which was under Austrian suzerainty.

Marek puckered his lips, licked them, and at the same time managed to whisper in such a way that no one looking at him could have discerned it. "And Zakonski, he is not to be trusted either."

The immediate question Henry would have liked to have asked of course, was, why not? He contented himself by simply raising an eyebrow. That Marek should be warning him against a fellow Pole struck Henry as strange. Had Zakonski gone against the grain of the Polish nobility and not supported Bonaparte? Or was it some particular intrigue wholly unconnected?

"Everyone in this city has a hidden agenda," Marek whispered. "Not all of them are legal. Or moral."

Henry pulled at his cuffs, thought how thankful he was to be there as a guest of Marek's. Count Ralenski won friends through his easy demeanor and it was universally acknowledged that he was first and foremost a Pole, but beyond that it seemed he only ever took sides at the card table.

The countess spoke to each of her guests in turn, he noticed, sharing a few words or a joke with them, and then moving seamlessly on to the next. Henry discovered that he could surreptitiously regard her from a variety of angles using the numerous mirrors that lined the walls of the room while still appear to be listening to the convoluted and improbable hunting story one of the Russians was telling. Henry allowed himself a small smile.

"What amuses you?" Marek asked, raising his chin. "The sight of all these men paying court to one woman?"

"Yes, perhaps." Henry shrugged his shoulders. Ralenski was perceptive, although "amused" was not quite how he would describe it.

When at last she moved towards them, their tight circle parted like the Red Sea. The Russians on one side, the Poles on the other and Henry left standing somewhere in the middle.

Henry traced the line of her décolletage. She wore a very low cut gown, the silk sitting so comfortably against the skin it was easy enough to imagine it was not there at all.

He breathed in the soft swell of her chest, marked the faint flush that danced up her collarbone. Henry smiled to himself. He'd seen enough female trickery in the ballrooms of Europe to last him a lifetime. It was quite natural he found her attractive of course, just as many a man might admire an expertly painted picture.

She spoke to the Russians first and, he was surprised to hear, in their own language. When she came to him, the sound of her speaking in English startled him.

"Mr. Champion, I am delighted that you have accepted my hospitality."

"Countess, your servant," he replied.

Did she imagine it, or had a small flicker of surprise passed across Mr. Champion's face when she spoke to him? She had known he would come with Ralenski of course. Annabel held up her hand. He bowed over it and kissed it in the English style, holding her wrist as delicately as if it were porcelain, brushing his lips almost imperceptibly over the silk of her gloves. He was so very similar to how she remembered: tall, handsome, with his hair still thick on top and cut in a slightly unruly style so that small curls brushed the sides of his ears and the top of his cravat. The only sign that ten years had passed were the tiny, fine lines at the outer edges of his eyes.

"I wish to converse with you on a number of subjects," she said, and hoped that she sounded suitably vague to anyone who might overhear. "But not tonight."

She observed his eyes narrow for a moment. He was probably wondering why she did not mention Lord and Lady Roseley to him, which would be the natural thing to do. She smiled but he did not relax. He seemed taut, from the way he held his shoulders to the way he held his glass, like a pulled spring.

If only he knew how she felt inside: like a butter churn. She needed to keep their conversation brief, and unremarkable. "How are you enjoying our city, Mr. Champion?"

"A great deal, although I have not been here very long." He coughed and broke her gaze.

"Krakow is a great Polish city," she continued. "In the peace settlement, while the rest of the historic nation of Poland has been given into Russian, Prussian and Austrian hands, the city of Krakow has had the good fortune to become an island on its own, a self-governing free city. You must see the castle while you are here, where the Polish kings are buried."

"Indeed," he replied, his gaze fixed on her pearls around her neck.

"I'm afraid there are many people I must talk to tonight." She gave a laugh. He probably knew it was a little forced. "Will you come tomorrow? So that we may converse... about England?"

He looked up. His eyes pierced her, deep splinters of brown within darker flecks. Eyes that showed there was much more to the very ordinary Mr. Champion that perhaps she had ever really credited. He nodded and spoke without emotion. "Yes, Countess, I will come tomorrow."

Chapter Four

Annabel had a moment, a step, to compose her thoughts. Not long enough. They were in complete disarray. He had unnerved her.

In her mind's eye remained her impression of Mr. Champion. He had a steady, reflective face framed with Anglo-Saxon blond curls, atop a sturdy, athletic frame. A man you expected to discover hunted hard, fenced, yet this was somewhat tempered by his height and the excellent cut of his clothes.

Nothing about him, however, was as arresting as his eyes. They were hazel-colored, like the spring hare, and equally as lively. They never seemed to leave her no matter where she was in the room. They still probably watched her now.

She needed this Englishman to help her, not send unwanted tremors down her spine. She had wondered how it would feel on meeting him again. Now she knew, and it was much more real, and much more frightening than she could have predicted. Time was supposed to diminish, was it not? Not make feelings grow.

Dear heavens, please let it not complicate the possibility that he might be able to help her, nothing to cloud her judgment. Please.

"Countess." Zakonski bent down and kissed her hand. It took every ounce of her willpower not to snatch her hand away. Annabel chided herself. Nothing substantial had changed in the last few minutes. She still held her fan in her left hand, her head high.

"Count, what a pleasure to see you in Krakow," she said although to be polite to him went against every grain.

"Thank you, and it is a pleasure to see you also." Zakonski smiled like the serpent from the Garden of Eden. "I look forward to renewing our acquaintance."

Could she just half-nod, pretend to be distracted by the next conversation, move on without having to reply or properly acknowledge what he had just said? She looked around.

"Countess?" He raised an eyebrow.

She had hesitated too long and missed her chance. She willed her voice to sound light and carefree. "I had thought you would remain in the country awhile?"

"I have no other pressing business," he replied. His eyes narrowed.

"Please excuse me." Annabel swept away to greet the next guests in a single determined movement she hoped he could not interrupt.

He did not and she passed into the next group. Annabel cast a glance backwards after a few moments and saw that Count Zakonski was engaged in conversation elsewhere. He did not turn or acknowledge that she was looking at him and she turned back to her companions with some feeling of relief. She was being fanciful. He might be back in Krakow and she might be forced to entertain him, but could do nothing with all these people here.

****

"You've now met all the people you don't want to meet in this city, Henry," Marek said an hour later once they had left the countess's house and were walking back down *Ulica Szpitalna* towards the main market square on their way to dine at a restaurant.

It had rained and the scattering of clouds had moved on, leaving the sky a deep gray blanket. The streets glistened from the lamplight and the light from the moon.

"Charmed I am sure," Henry agreed. If the countess's reception was about politics then it was politics that relied on coded language or other subtleties because he'd not been aware of any conversations he would describe as political. But then Krakow's status of free city had only been finally signed in November. Perhaps it was early days in terms of political intrigues.

"I don't know what we were doing there except that the countess wants to talk to you about England. I don't know if she is after anything from me. I was a friend of her husband's but..."

"You were?" Henry had not realized this. At some time he would have to confide his true purpose with regards to the countess. He was sure that Marek could be trusted, but he would rather make sure to have spoken to her first and secured her agreement to return with him to England before he said anything to Marek. "What happened to her husband?" he asked.

"Did I not tell you?" Marek sounded surprised.

"No."

"Ah, then you had better be told. He was killed." Marek tapped his cane on the ground. "In a duel."

"Oh. Oh, dear."

"And can you guess who the other duelist was?"

"No." What a strange question Marek asked. How the devil should he know?

"Henry, you've not been paying attention! You met him this evening. Can you not guess?"

Henry looked down, saw the cobbles below their feet shining a silvery gray, disappearing all too rapidly under the blackness of their footsteps. He couldn't see how he was supposed to know which of the gentlemen at dinner had dueled with the countess's husband. If he was forced to hazard a guess he would have put his money on Count Zakonski. There was an uneasiness between him and the countess which was more than predatory male and unwilling female.

But it was none of his business to guess.

"No, I can't guess," Henry said.

Marek rapped his cane against a stone step. "Count Zakonski, of course."

Henry stopped. So did the shadows, and a half-moment later, Marek. The words ran repeatedly, like the patter of mice, through Henry's head; Zakonski had killed the countess's husband in a duel.

"What was the duel about?" Henry heard himself ask, saw in his mind's eye the image of Zakonski, his teeth flashing, his eyebrows hunched, as bushy as a boar's fur.

"Land." Marek shrugged his shoulders. "A minor, but not unusual feud between Polish families. Rather unfortunate that events turned out as they did as Szalynski was a good fellow. You would have liked him." He clapped Henry on the back. "Come on. Let's get ourselves dinner and a slug of something strong? It's late and there is nowhere else to go in this place at this hour, unless you want a card table or a whore's bed?"

"No, thank you." Henry shook his head, pleased to count neither of those vices as his own these days. "Dinner is enough for me."

"Good," Marek replied. "I'm hungry."

Henry gave a jaunty whistle and the cold air tickled his teeth. There was no need to let Marek think that his interest in the duel meant anything more to him than an amusing conversation aside.

Why had the countess even received the man? There was more going on here, Henry was sure, than met the eye. The duel had not been about the countess then, or had it? Sometimes what a duel was fought on was just the excuse, and a woman was the oldest one in the book.

Henry stuffed his hands in the pockets of his cape, his fingers were feeling numb, quickened his stride to match Marek's who was forging on ahead. He did not like the idea that the duel might have been about the countess.

How foolish he was! She was nothing to him. Nothing, save a way to earn back his inheritance, and repay Jonathan Harvey in some small way by being of service to old friends of his father.

****

Annabel let the curtain drop back from where she had parted it with her hand a fraction to watch her guests spill out into the street.

At least, thank heavens, they were now gone. She picked up the crystal glass of water from the tray a servant had just brought her and found her hands were shaking. She put the glass back down, staggered back, and sat in the first chair. Anything to steady herself. She forced in a few deep breaths.

The immediate relief died. That other emotion, the one even stronger and always present with her, every day, rose up like acid bile in her throat: fear.

She felt cold as a stone. She held her hands together and saw that the tips of her fingers were white. The stove in the corner of the salon had been well stoked, had it not? She got up and opened the iron door carefully to check. Inside fire was blazing. She closed the door. The stove went from floor to ceiling, completely tiled. She put a hand within an inch of the tiles: they were too warm to touch.

The candles were burning, reflecting their lights into every corner of the room from the mirrors behind them on the walls. Her salon. A room she had modeled in the French Bourbon style. A room fit for nobles and princes. And with the mirrors wherever she was standing she could catch every movement, every expression. One room where she thought she would be safe.

Count Zakonski had arrived and the simple fact of his presence was enough to strip it all away. What was he doing here? What did he want?

A gentle tap at the door. It was her maid, Helena, with a taper in case she wished to retire. She did. Though, with her mind as it was now, would she ever sleep?

Annabel nodded and thanked Helena, who left the taper on a side cabinet and disappeared.

Annabel rose, collected the taper, and paused before she left the room; who could she trust?

Count Ralenski? She might be able to trust Ralenski, maybe. She pondered on it all the way upstairs to her chamber. He had been friends with her husband and he was also friends with, or at least in the same circle as, Prince Czartoryski. Ralenski was also one of the few people who knew most of the truth of what had happened and he had not spilled a word of it to anyone to her knowledge. She also knew there was little love lost between him and Zakonski. But as to Ralenski's game, of that she was not sure. Surely it was not entirely safe for him to be in Krakow? She would not have thought he was entirely safe, not the way things were, with him having fought for Napoleon. Loyalties seemed to shift in this city, like sand.

Her chamber was as warm as toast compared to the draughty corridor, and Annabel shut the heavy door thankfully. She knew that it was far safer to play her own game and trust no one until she could be absolutely sure.

The stove had been lit some time and Helena would have taken the chill off the bed with the warming pan that was now re-hung on the wall.

Annabel slid her hand under the counterpane. Yes, the bed had been warmed. And it was always possible that fate might be smiling on her for a change because fate had instructed her dear aunt and uncle to arrange someone to rescue her home, and that person was Mr. Champion.

She would get ready for bed quickly, before it cooled. She usually undressed herself. The Empire style had practically done away with the need for a maid, the gowns were so simply fastened and her figure did not require stays.

She found herself thinking, as she lay in bed, about what really had attracted her to Mr. Champion in the first place. Perhaps it was his earnestness? He had seemed a person of substance, a rare species against a backdrop of fops, dandies and weak-willed young gentlemen she had come to be surrounded by during her debut in London. But she had rejected him—though she'd seen the seemingly paradoxical twins, passion and steadfastness, burn in his eyes—because he was too ordinary. He had no title. His family was of no consequence.

After the debacle with Freddie, she'd turned her sights instead on Count Szalynski who had already shown her some interest, and determined to catch a husband, she had caught him. Their courtship had been brief and they were married, a quickly-arranged affair, in time for her to travel back with him to the Continent. She had not thought then that she would be away from England so long. She had spent the first weeks of her marriage in Paris. A wonderful time, she had visited dressmakers, the Opera, and started to relish the freedom of being a married woman rather than a debutante. They honeymooned properly in the Italian Lakes and there she discovered what a real wife's duties were about. When she refused to share his bed, he had grown very angry. It was a white anger, that seemed unnaturally cool, and he did not force her. Instead

45

he said, "You are no true wife to me," and took a succession of mistresses. He was very discreet yet it hurt for a long time, until she came to the decision one day that weeping would never do any good, and after that he started to treat her better and they became, in a peculiar way, friends.

Szalynski had always maintained that the English political system was the model that the world should follow. England ruled her Empire not through the application of force and fervor but with *trust, commerce and a few ships*. It reflected how he dealt with others around him. Not only her, but when they returned to Poland and found that Count Zakonski had taken control of the Szalynski lands and castle in Galicia, he'd taken Zakonski straight to court. At the same time, he campaigned in the locality, whipping up support for the Szalynski cause and making sure that Zakonski was paid the worst prices year after year for his harvests. The court hesitated over their decision. Szalynski had pressed. Three years later the court ruled in his favor and Zakonski had been forced to quit the castle. Szalynski held a series of banquets, patched up the cottages of the peasants which had been allowed to decay and had started on an extensive program of improvements. Annabel had suggested running a school for local children and he had supported her in every way.

Annabel found herself smiling at the memory of her late husband's face and his actions so very much in earnest. Even though she had been far younger than him, she had married at seventeen, he'd come to treat her as a sentient being. One able to grasp the concepts of the machinations of the states of Europe and the cause Count Szalynski had supported all his life—an independent Polish nation. Were he alive now he would have no doubt done what his friend Koscuiszko had done; curse the

Vienna settlement that had placed the greater part of the Polish nation under Russian suzerainty and retire to Switzerland in disgust.

The face she saw in her mind that replaced her husband's countenance was not Koscuiszko's, the broken hero, but Mr. Champion's.

She liked his face, but it would not do to judge by appearances or make assumptions based on their brief encounter years ago. She had to discover whether she could fully trust him. And not let her judgment be clouded by that tingling emotion that drew her towards him as any weak woman to an attractive man.

Chapter Five

It looked to be another bright day. Sunlight streamed through the tall windows and bathed his chamber in lemon yellow. Spring was kicking winter away. Henry folded his arms where he stood with the sun warming his back and decided that he was right in thinking there was no rush to go anywhere else or back to England. The situation here looked not to be as simple as it seemed.

"I expect we will stay here at least another month," he said to Robards, his manservant. He needed to get to know Countess Szalynski better, which would begin this morning. And then resolve this little difficulty with her late husband's lands, at least as far as to enable her to feel she could leave Poland.

"I'd better try and learn s'more Polish then, sir." Robards lifted a freshly laundered cravat from the pile in the drawer and, as was his habit, examined it minutely for any defect.

Henry waited patiently, recalling item by item every detail of Countess Szalynski. Her dark hair, arranged simply, her stunning blue eyes. What she had been wearing last night.

"Yes, I suppose it's dashed difficult in the servants hall is it?" he said. His memory had reached her décolletage, and was about to embark on shameful invention unless he put a halt to it now. "I don't suppose anyone speaks English at all?"

Robards looked up and shook his head. "But I understand right enough what's going on. I think I've picked up quite a few words actually. From one of the footmen, the tall one with the long thin nose, Lech his name is. He's been trying to teach me Polish and I have been teaching 'im some English. You know, point at summit and then say the word, like? And then he writes it down too, in me notebook." Robards patted his chest with his right hand and Henry could just discern the outline of what could be a small notebook in the inside pocket.

"But it's all them z's that get me," Robards added. He smoothed his hand over the cravat and smiled.

"Hmmm, while you're at it, you can teach me a few words." Henry lifted his chin so Robards could attend to the procedure of tying the cravat now it had passed muster.

"Well, for starters this here cravat, that's called a *krawat*, but you roll your 'r' a little more when you say it, sir. And it is written K-R-A-W-A-T. If you see a w, that is always pronounced like a v. Useful to know that, sir."

"W's are v's, I'll remember that. Like the Wawel castle, it is pronounced with v's but written with w's."

"Yes, sir. Very good, sir." Robards folded the linen around his neck and began the task of intricately knotting it in the English style.

"You got your German up to scratch, didn't you?" Henry mumbled knowing it wasn't worth moving an inch at this critical point in the procedure. If Robards tied the knot even slightly awry he wouldn't be satisfied and he'd toss the offending linen away and reach for a fresh one and begin all over again.

"Yes, sir. There, done. Not bad at all if I say so myself."

Robards had taken a step back to survey his handiwork and Henry glanced down from the ceiling and straightened his neck. The cravat was the very last item of his attire to get right and now he was dressed to face the day. "But don't any of the servants here speak German?"

"Yes, one of the maids, Maria, she speaks German." Robards had the decency to blush. "I think some of 'er family might be Austrian, sir."

"So you aren't completely without conversation?" Henry fought to keep a smile off his face.

"You haven't met Maria, sir? I'll tell you I don't want to be having too many conversations with 'er or I'll find m'self being hauled away to meet 'er father, so to speak."

"Oh, I see." Henry straightened his shoulders and glanced at himself in the mirror as a final check. "Well, Robards, you must of course do as you see fit, but I shall be most distressed to lose such a fine manservant. If it comes to it, perhaps this Maria could come back with us to England."

Robards grimaced. "Like I say, sir, you haven't met 'er. Right scared of 'er I am to be honest."

Henry chuckled. He'd never thought he'd see the day when his savvy manservant who had trudged half the length and breadth of Spain on campaign facing the enemy on so many occasions would be scared of a bit of skirt.

****

There was a woman selling flowers from a stall in *Rynek Glowny*, the main market square, and the thought crossed Henry's mind that perhaps he should bring the countess as a small gift a posy of spring flowers. Nothing extravagant. He paused in front of the stall and perused the various baskets full of flowers before deciding against it. Even if it was the custom here to bring flowers on very ordinary visits one didn't do so under the same circumstances in England and he was an Englishman going to visit an Englishwoman.

He didn't want her to get the wrong idea, not a woman who may have had many lovers and admirers. She might expect…

…that he had come with a certain intent.

Henry turned on his heels abruptly, sending a pair of pigeons flapping away half-heartedly into the sky. He would write a page or two about the flower seller and the daily scene in the main square in his notebook later. Keeping up the fiction that he was writing a book was hard work, but it was a convenient excuse to Marek for his particular interest in coming to Krakow. In some ways he was enjoying putting his thoughts and observations down on paper.

He walked past St. Mary's church, and through the little square before turning left onto *Ulica Szpitalna*. It was a longer route but Henry had decided to come this way rather than risk venturing alone down any more alleyways, even though it was broad daylight.

He felt a small prickle at the back of his neck. He could do without being accosted by any more footpads.

****

"Countess, your servant." Henry bowed, but moderately. "Good morning."

Annabel snatched her hand away from where she had been fiddling with the pearls in her necklace. "Mr. Champion, how kind of you to call."

She stood up, straight, brushed her hands down the front of her skirts. She had not had time to compose herself properly, had not expected him to come quite so early. He stood there, bright as a buckle, when other men would still be sleeping off the excesses of the night before in their beds.

"Your invitation was most clear, Countess," he said. There was a sparkle in his eye.

She could see him much better in the daylight, and was surprised to see he didn't need the luster of candlelight to be kind to his complexion. There was nothing harsh about it, no lines or marks, nor flushes of color suggesting he enjoyed his drink too much. If he'd been an acquaintance of long standing she'd have told him he looked a picture of health.

"Do sit down, Mr. Champion." She moved over to the damask upholstered chaise. Sometimes with gentlemen she lingered on her feet, allowed them to greet her with a kiss on the hand. Not this one. His lips had brushed her fingers last night, and even though they had been gloved it disturbed her.

"Thank you," he said.

He was watching her as she sat down. Annabel placed her hands elegantly on her lap. She must sit still and not to let him see she was trembling slightly. She wanted to chide herself. She could not explain why this man should make her feel so but it seemed a weakness that she felt as she did.

He flicked his coat and sat opposite her on the red chaise. She'd had it made recently, a copy of a French piece she had seen in one of the staterooms at the Wawel castle. It suited him, framed his figure, and allowed him to lean back slightly without looking disordered.

"I must thank you for last night, Countess. It was a most pleasant evening and my compliments to your chef."

"I am pleased to hear you enjoyed it."

"Might I compliment you on your command of languages, Countess?"

"You may, Mr. Champion."

"For my own part I can only speak French passably." He stretched his long legs out further, if that was possible. "And only a very little German," he added in a lazy drawl. "I suppose I should try a little harder. It would be most useful on one's travels."

She liked the sound of his timbre. She'd not really noticed it before but it had been so noisy here last night. The morning was still, with nothing to compete against the smooth sound of his voice except the gentle tick of the French porcelain clock and the soft crackle of the fire.

"Thank you, Mr. Champion, but I am fortunate that imitation comes naturally to me and language has held a fascination for me since I was a child."

His serious-looking eyes caught hers. "You could teach me Polish," he said, "but I promise I would be a very bad scholar."

Annabel swallowed, broke his gaze, and felt her heart racing out of control. Something quite unexplainable just swept through her, a quiver, startled her by its force. Could it possibly have been caused by just one look?

"You are not here for Polish lessons, Mr. Champion," she said, refolding her hands in her lap. She hoped he hadn't noticed how he had so easily thrown her off balance. "You are here so we might talk about England."

"Quite right," he replied, seemingly unperturbed by anything. "In any case I don't require Polish lessons, my valet is teaching me."

"Your valet? Is he Polish?" Annabel snatched her hand away from her pearls again. How it had managed to wander up there without noticing she didn't know. She forced her errant fingers to grip the ruby ring she wore, her mother's ring.

"No, my man Robards is a Londoner born and bred."

"And what has he taught you?" Annabel could not help asking. The twists this conversation had taken were most extraordinary.

Mr. Champion smiled. "Krawat," he said with a passable imitation of a Polish accent.

"Bravo!" Annabel clapped her hands together and thought she might really collapse with laughter were it not that her eyes were drawn to his neckcloth and she stilled. It was pristine and, she had to admit, surely added to his handsomeness. A stark white bed for his firm chin to rest, along with the lowest golden curls of his hair. "I understood you perfectly, Mr. Champion."

His brow creased and he sat up and leaned forward. She thought he might reach out and clasp her hands in his own, try to touch her in some way. They were not sitting so very far apart.

Her breath caught.

He didn't.

He sat there, poised yet still. His eyes flickered as he watched her.

Annabel blinked and chided herself. She must be imagining things. Living as she did played constant tricks on her mind. She might be walking down the street, safely flanked by her maid and a footman and still think she could discern figures about to leap out from the shadows.

"Countess, what would you like to know of England? Much has happened since you left, though no doubt you have heard all the news. A prime minister assassinated, a king gone mad. Troubles with machine-breaking. The abolition of the slave trade. War."

"Many things." Her voice quivered and she knew that a clever man such as he would notice that and also the unaccountable delay in her reply while she'd been lost in her thoughts. "It has been a long time since-"

They were interrupted by a knock on the door.

"Please excuse me," Annabel said to her guest and then bid the footman enter. He carried a tray on which sat a large coffee pot, two China cups and an assortment of pastries. "I hope you will take coffee. I asked for it to be served as soon as you arrived. It is a little early but..."

"I like coffee very much," Mr. Champion replied

and shifted slightly so he sat more upright.

The footman placed the tray down on the small low table by her side.

"The fashion here is to serve our coffee very much in what is called the Viennese style." Annabel pointed to the small jug and pot. "With cream and sugar. Although it was in fact a Pole who established the first coffee house in Vienna."

"Is that so? How interesting."

She saw in the mirror that his eyes were fixed on watching her pour the coffee, add the cream and the sugar and stir it for him with the small silver spoon. Why were her hands shaking? She had managed to pour, got this far without a hitch but the cup rattled on its saucer as she picked it up and leaned forward to hand it to him.

"Thank you," he said and slid his fingers underneath the saucer and clenched it in his firm grasp.

Annabel breathed evenly again. The moment when they'd both been holding his cup had followed the heart stopping moment she'd thought, in her foolishness, she might drop it.

Their fingers had not even touched.

For which she should be thankful or she might well have dropped the cup and sent his coffee spilling over her Persian carpet.

He placed his cup down on the table beside his chaise and she attended to her own coffee.

"I expect that you know all about Waterloo, the restoration in France and the Vienna peace settlement," he said. "The impact on England has been that it has made Wellington a national hero, a new Nelson. And because the continental blockades have finished, so gentlemen do not have to rely on smugglers to bring them French brandy and wines, and the ladies may travel safely to Paris once more for the fashions, and to Switzerland and Italy for their health."

Annabel looked up, caught his watchful gaze and returned her eyes swiftly to the cream and sugar. "I have never been to the Alps," she muttered, "but I have heard they are very picturesque."

He leaned forward. "Countess, but might I take a moment to consider the aspect from your windows?" he spoke with a voice as soft as feathers.

"Please," she said, confused for a moment as to what had driven him to make such a strange request. He could wander over to the window now for some moments, with his back to her, and he did, and she would have some privacy to compose herself.

By way of manners it was clear he was a gentleman of the first order.

And she was nervous. She had built this Englishman up so much in her mind as a man who could help her, she had placed too much on this meeting. She needed to cast that all aside now and consider what she needed to find out. About him, his background, his character. She couldn't rely on what she distantly remembered from ballrooms in England so many years ago. She needed to establish whether he was trustworthy, and as soon as she could steer the subject in that direction, she must do so.

"And your verdict on the aspect, Mr. Champion?" she asked after some moments.

"There is good light," he said, "and you have a clear view, but the street needs some repair as does the building directly opposite."

Exactly what sort of man came to your house and discerned the aspect from your best room? Annabel felt something warm in her chest. It was surely better than the usual platitudes.

"Do come and sit down, Mr. Champion, if you have finished."

"Thank you," he replied.

It was a pleasure to watch him stalk back to the red chaise and settle himself down again. He caught her eye and smiled at her. "If I may be frank with you—"

There was another tap at the door.

Annabel started, wondered what it could be. She bid in Polish that the servant enter.

It was another visitor. At this time in the morning? Annabel enquired of her servant who it was and Count Zakonski was the reply. A shiver, like a small animal with tiny clawed feet, ran down her back. "Tell him I am not at home," she said in Polish.

"I had better leave you to attend to your new visitor," Mr. Champion said.

"No, please stay," Annabel replied. "I am not... at home to the other visitor."

She noticed his reaction: one of surprise. She struggled to think what to say. "I did not wish to receive the visitor who called, that is all."

Why? His eyes said. "I visited your aunt and uncle before I left England. They were both very much looking forward to your return to England."

Annabel looked up but the servant had gone. Still, she could not be sure who might be listening at doors. She leaned forward, so close that she could hear Mr. Champion's deep, even breathing. She swallowed and willed her heart to beat less quickly. She spoke in a low voice not much above a whisper. "We cannot talk about this now. Here. But we must talk. Soon. I shall arrange it." No response. Then, he nodded. She raised her voice. "Thank you, Mr. Champion. It has been most enjoyable that you could visit and I hope to see you again soon."

He smiled and their eyes held for a moment longer than they should have.

"Yes...yes, I did so want to ask you about England," she said and folded and then refolded her hands on her lap. A blush rose on her cheeks, she seemed flustered. Had catching his eye really affected her that much? Henry felt his own heart beating slightly faster than it should.

"We didn't manage to talk much about England. Shall I call again? Are you usually at home in the morning...or in the afternoon?"

"In the morning," she replied and rose to her feet. "I look forward to it, Mr. Champion."

"I will not deny, Countess, that the prospect also pleases me." He would kiss her hand, he decided, and stepped towards her.

"The school you went to, did they teach you this charm?"

"No," he murmured, lifting her hand to his lips, "the ballrooms of Europe."

"Thank you for calling, Mr. Champion," she said looking up at him and leaving her hand rested on his fingers a little too long.

"Until we meet again." He bowed before leaving her.

Chapter Six

He found Marek in the sitting room on the first floor of his house that overlooked the quiet courtyard at the back.

"Ah, Henry, good morning." Marek looked up from the journal he'd been reading. Marek's house was around three hundred years old, built like so many of the grand town houses in the Renaissance style and comprised a rather odd collection of rooms. There were three sitting rooms altogether but Marek seemed to prefer this one despite its small size. Perhaps because it got the best light in the morning.

"Good morning, Marek." Henry flipped his coat tails and sat down on one of the ancient chairs opposite.

"How was the visit? A success? Does the Countess Szalynski now know everything she requires about recent events in England?"

"My visit was cut rather short actually. Count Zakonski arrived and I thought it better to leave."

"You were wise." Marek's lips curved into a smile. "I always think when that man comes into a room it is like... like a bad smell coming in."

"Is he an... intimate friend of the countess?"

"Intimate? What do you mean, Henry?" Marek raised an eyebrow.

"Are they... are they lovers?" There, he had said it. Henry unclenched his fingers from digging into his palms.

"Lovers?" Marek started laughing so hard Henry thought he might fall off his sofa.

"What's so amusing?"

"Sorry, friend," Marek replied trying to recover himself. He bashed his fist against the cushion at his side, sending a cloud of dust into the air.

Henry struggled to wrest his handkerchief from his top pocket in time and sneezed.

"This place is full of damn dust," Marek said, tears still streaming down his cheeks.

Henry blew his nose and tucked his handkerchief away. "No matter."

"It does matter. Servants have been lazy while I've been gone." Marek smiled. "Anyway, she wouldn't bed that cur Zakonski in a hundred years. Unless he forced her."

Something unpleasant gripped Henry in the gut.

"I wouldn't put that past him, you know," Marek continued, his face sober. "Anyhow, why do you want to know?"

"I simply wondered," Henry replied. He was hungry, wasn't he? That was the explanation behind the spasm in his stomach. He hadn't been in a humor to eat breakfast this morning. The countess's love affairs were nothing to him. "You said last night not to trust him."

"Yes, what you say is interesting. I was wondering last night what Zakonski was doing here in Krakow. In fact I was making some enquiries on that very subject this morning. He is only renting a house here. His estates are some two days ride south in Galicia. Certainly do not trust him with anything. Please take my word for this, Henry. The man is a law unto himself, I think you call it?"

"Ah, I see. Outside the law."

"However," Marek creased his brow in concentration, "we keep Zakonski our friend, for now. It all gets complicated, and you understand that some of this political stuff I cannot even speak to you of it? Even though I would trust you with my life."

Henry nodded. He got the strong impression that Zakonski and Marek had different political agendas. Marek had been a Bonapartist and was certainly a Polish nationalist. It would seem most likely, therefore, that Zakonski was not.

"We go tonight to Zakonski's to play cards. Two bits of advice. Don't play him, he probably cheats. Like those Belgians we played against in Vienna. Remember?" Marek grinned.

"Don't remind me."

"And don't play me," Marek added, his grin widening. "It will cost you more than you expect!"

"Yes." Henry smiled in return. He knew he could play a shrewd game but Marek's ability exceeded his own and, because his own pockets were so shallow, serious gambling was out of the question. "Now I had better go and scribble down a few of my observations from today or this damn book will never get written!"

Henry wandered upstairs and sat down at the escritoire in his room. He opened the small leather bound book in which he was making notes onto a new page and shook his pen before unscrewing the cap of his ink pot.

In his bold, well schooled hand he wrote about a dozen lines about Krakow's main market square, the main buildings of interest, the churches, the cloth hall, the merchants' houses and then a few lines about the vendors to be found there including the flower sellers.

Then he put his pen away. That he should have something written was important, in case Marek ever asked to see this book of his. Right now, he wanted some time alone to think. He was going to have to be frank with her tomorrow and explain to her that the Roseley's had placed her under his protection. It was imperative that she explain to him the situation with Zakonski or any other difficulties

she might be in.
****

Darkness fell on the city like a smothering blanket. They talked of improvements: pulling down the old medieval walls to create a circular boulevard of a park, a natural, green, living ribbon around the old town. The streets, busy in the day, grew quiet. An occasional carriage broke the dulling silence. Irregular watchmen lit the sparse lamps. The few figures who went abroad moved through the shadows soundlessly. Only the boots of nobles clicked on the stone paving.

Annabel reached into the very back of her wardrobe and pulled out a long black cloak. It was pristine. Oh, bother! Helena must have found it and cleaned it.

She threw it on the floor and then went over to the hearth, took a poker from the rack and pushed some of the ash and charred debris from the edge of the grate so it fell on the stone flags below.

She waited for them to cool.

Annabel paced over to the window, pushed aside the curtain so that she could look onto the dark, empty street below.

What was Zakonski doing in Krakow? He'd taken a house on *Ulica Kanonicza* so she had heard. For how long, she didn't know. Or whether he had leased the house or purchased it. It had been empty for a while that house, and before that it was lived in by a late professor of the Krakow Academy.

After a couple of minutes she let the curtain fall and went back to the stove. It was vital she discerned Zakonski's purpose in coming to Krakow without delay.

She opened the stove which had not been lit since last night. She pushed a finger gingerly into the ash. It was cold. She bent down properly, scooped up the ash and cinders in her cupped hands and threw them onto the cloak. Stooped, she rubbed some of the scattered gray flecks into the black material.

Once she was satisfied the cloak was soiled enough she collected the remainder of the ash and consulting with the mirror on the dressing table stroked it carefully across every inch of her face. She took one of the large pieces of charcoal and crushed it with the spare bone from an altered stay she kept in a drawer. She swabbed the powder across her neck and behind her ears, smudged it under her eyes and on the tip of her nose for good measure.

There was a tap as quiet as a mouse on her door.

Helena crept in also dressed in a long black cloak. She stopped and stared.

"Do you not like my make-up?" Annabel asked.

"You look a mess!" Helena bent down and picked the cloak up from the floor, her eyes wide. "What's this? Ash from the stove?"

"Good!" Annabel stood up and took the cloak from her before Helena could start brushing it. "I certainly did not want to be mistaken for a lady of the night. You are going visiting but I want to fade into the background as an old crone, of no interest to anyone."

Annabel donned the cloak, pulled the hood up and Helena helped her to do up every fastening so every inch of her apart from her face was covered. Her outfit was completed by an ancient pair of half boots any self-respecting lady would have given away years ago.

The half boots were a risk but it wasn't beyond the realms of possibility that a lady's cast-offs might end up in the hands of an old woman, and the half boots had soft soles. She would make hardly any noise as she walked through the cobbled streets.

"I am ready," Annabel said taking one last glance at herself in the mirror and picking up a

taper. Helena went around the room snuffing all the candles out. "Let's go."
****

He'd been in gambling hells where the play was less vicious than in here, Henry mused. He watched the Russian opposite him without even a flicker of emotion gather up the enormous pile of notes and coins, including the two *louis d'or* that had come from his own pocket. As a stranger here he felt obliged to play with real money: gold you could bite your teeth on as one fellow had indeed taken the liberty of doing. But the stakes were getting too high for his liking.

Henry coughed involuntarily. He really must get out of here: the air didn't move, the smoke hung. He pushed his chair back, excused himself from the play. It seemed a good moment. Not that he cared much about losing the money. It was more that he could do without becoming known as the Englishman with a bottomless pocket of gold.

He hadn't come to this party of Zakonski's to play cards. Nor had a lot of other guests, Henry noticed as he walked out of the long salon and into Zakonski's vast hallway, a room in its own right. The air was clearer here too. The double height ceiling dissipated the smoke from the cigarillos. Henry breathed thankfully.

The room was broken at even intervals with half-columns pressed against the wall, a late gesture to fashion as the house was far older than the neo-classical modeling of the inside suggested. In front of each column stood elegant *egalitaires*, such as you would commonly find in Paris, and on top of them large Dresden vases containing ferns.

The room perfectly designed for small intimate conversations to take place at intervals and in every space, Henry observed that this was indeed what was going on. He spied Hantenberg, the Austrian, in a group of four men and walked over to them, wondering how he could inveigle himself in their conversation.

Henry walked towards them, tried to pick up the tread of what they were talking about as he approached. They were speaking in French so chances were the men were not all Austrian like Hantenberg or he would have expected them to speak German. From what Henry gathered, it was about furs, the import of furs from Russia. They were discussing prices. It sounded as if a deal was being cut.

One of the men drew out his snuff box as Henry was only a foot away. *Voila*! His chance to interrupt. But how he hated snuff.

"I couldn't by any chance trouble you for a pinch?" Henry said. "Quite run out myself."

"Certainly," the man said, handing him the small enamel box.

"Thank you very much," Henry said and helped himself to the smallest amount he thought he could get away with. He balanced it on the side of his forefinger, tipped his head back, and inhaled violently.

He smiled. Heavens, he had to do something with his features that were threatening a grimace.

"Much obliged," Henry said.

"Mr. Champion, isn't it?" Hantenberg leaned forward. "I believe we met at the Countess Szalynski's the other night?"

"Indeed we did!" Henry responded enthusiastically. Wait, he had better pretend their brief introduction had meant very little to him. "Count, er...?"

"Count von Hantenberg." The count's eyes narrowed. "May I introduce you to the company?"

"Delighted," Henry said. The strong smelling weed was tickling his nose like the very devil.

Heavens, he wasn't going to sneeze was he? He tried to fix all their names and faces even though his eyes were still smarting. Hantenberg's business was with a Russian, a Ukrainian and a Pole.

"And what brings you to Krakow?" Hantenberg said. "Business?"

"Pleasure," Henry replied with wave of his hand he hoped looked foppish. Hantenberg's question was not wholly unexpected but the way he asked it made Henry wonder. "Mostly pleasure, although I flatter myself I am dabbling at writing a book of my travels. I am here as the guest of my friend Count Ralenski."

"Have you traveled much, Mr. Champion? Have you by any chance been to Vienna?"

"Vienna? Of course! Why, I spent Christmas in Vienna." This interview was not going well at all. Hantenberg was curious, too curious. He needed to turn the tables, before he was forced into giving away too much. "Do you know the city well, Count von Hantenberg?"

"Know Vienna well? Or did you mean Krakow?" The count's gaze was piercing. Bells and whistles, he needed to turn this conversation to his advantage, and quickly.

"I was thinking of Vienna! But do you know Krakow well? Or are you, like me, only a visitor?"

"Merely a visitor," Hantenberg replied with an uneasy smile. He was lying, Henry could tell by the way his brows twitched and Hantenberg's gaze swept the ground as he spoke.

"Oh, please excuse me, gentlemen. It was a pleasure to make your acquaintance," Henry said and bowed formally. He withdrew from the group, walked away, towards Marek who he'd seen out of the corner of his eye emerging from the card salon.

Something bothered him about Hantenberg but he couldn't put a finger on it.
****

Annabel kept her cloak fastened tightly around her, her head down and implored Helena to do the same. If they were spotted, recognized, the plan would be ruined.

They skirted the shadowy perimeter of *Rynek Glowny* and walked briskly down *Ulica Grodzka* past the churches of Saints Peter and Paul and Saint Andrew and towards the Wawel hill.

It seemed to Annabel that the students of the Academy never slept and she slipped swiftly past the door to the *Collegium Juridicum* lest anyone suddenly emerge and by some chance recognize her before turning onto *Ulica Kanonicza*.

In the shadow of the Wawel cathedral and castle above, the very heart of the city, the heart of Poland, thought Annabel, nestled the many-windowed old merchant's house Zakonski rented. All three of its high stories towered over her. A proud, loyal house, Annabel decided as she looked up at it. She bit her tongue. She wanted to shout to the rooftops that he should not deserve the privilege of living here.

Next to the house was a small alley, down which was the back entrance of Zakonski's house: the entrance used by the servants.

She whispered Helena good luck and watched as her maid slipped away and tapped on a large black door.

After a couple of minutes it was opened and Helena stepped inside.

The door closed with a thud. Annabel shuddered, knew she must wait here alone until Helena returned, and hoped that she would not be long. Helena's cousin had been taken on as a kitchen maid. She had every reason to pay a casual visit to the house.

Annabel pressed her back against the plaster of the wall behind her and strained to see if she could hear any sounds coming from the house. Nothing. It was too cold to have windows open this late in the evening and the house wasn't one she knew. The reception rooms might well be situated upstairs and at the back.

It was cold for April. It was a strange time of year here in Poland. It could be spring one day and winter the next. Casting her gaze upwards to the sky she saw clouds and wondered if it might snow. It felt cold enough, out here in the dark night.

There was no one around and she stamped her feet together to warm them. She told herself sternly that she must find out what Zakonski was doing. Rather than lament the fact he had come to Krakow, she should regard it rather as a stroke of good fortune.

Helena had gone ahead but Annabel hoped it would be safe for her to be smuggled into the house too.

Could she get into Zakonski's study undiscovered? Find his writing desk unlocked? And would the papers be there? At the very least, she wanted to try and eavesdrop on the card party and a successful card evening could go on until dawn. If the coast was clear goodness knows what she might be able to discover. The thought warmed her.

****

"Henry!" Marek staggered towards him and hiccoughed.

"Are you drunk?" Henry asked in a low voice. He placed his hand on Marek's shoulder, guided him to one side of Zakonski's hallway, behind one of the *egaletaires*.

"No, just pretending," Marek said with a grin. "Opponents are more likely to make mistakes if they don't rate the opposition, don't you find?"

"You devious—"

"Ha! No worse than losing a few early games on purpose. Anyhow, you should see the play in there..."

"I have and my pockets are decidedly lighter. In fact I was thinking of wandering home?"

"Ah, well I shan't join you just yet. My little scheme has still to bear fruit."

"I've just been talking to Count von Hantenberg," Henry said keeping his tone even, disinterested.

Marek grimaced. "This is supposed to be a free city, Henry, the last part of Poland not to be controlled by foreigners, yet look about you! Men of every nationality plotting the making of a quick profit."

"Like Hantenberg?" Henry queried.

"Trade and commerce, destroys the soul of a place..." Marek's expression looked heavy suddenly. "Destroys the soul of a country. And the Poles are as eager as anyone to profit from the new opportunities, would rather join in than... than do anything to risk this new status quo. I don't know what I am doing here!"

What exactly was Marek doing in Krakow indeed? Another question Henry wanted the answer to. He hoped, very much hoped, his friend wasn't doing something incredibly foolish like trying to incite Polish nationalism. Bells and whistles, Henry thought, knowing Marek.

"Get back to the card table and I'll see you later," Henry said ducking around Marek.

"See you!" Marek replied, hiccoughed and winked.

Henry wandered swiftly towards the door. He simply needed to retrieve his coat.
****

Annabel stiffened at the sound of a long creak. A door opening? Her eyelids were heavy, she must have been standing here for at least half an hour.

Voices clipped the air.

"*Merci beaucoup.*"

"*Au reviour*, Monsieur."

It sounded as if the front door had opened and a guest was being shown out onto the street. She couldn't see from where she was standing.

A guest to whom French was not their first language. Nor Polish. And the voice sounded familiar.

Then she saw him, stepping into the middle of the street and into view, a tall figure, his back to her as he started to walk towards the *Collegium Juridicum*.

Not two paces had he gone when he stopped. "Now where the devil am I going?" he said to himself.

English? He turned. It was Mr. Champion. Her hand shot to her mouth.

Chapter Seven

Mr. Champion started heading towards her, the wrong way completely if he wished to get back to Count Ralenski's house. He should knock on Zakonski's door again and ask for directions rather than let himself get lost in a maze of dark streets. Annabel took a deep breath.

He didn't, he walked right past Zakonski's house. He began whistling. Annabel wanted to cradle her face in her hands. A sure invitation for every robber in town to try an easy picking.

She started at the sound of a door creaking, turned her head. Behind her two men had stepped into the alleyway from the back entrance to Zakonski's residence. They were dressed too roughly to be gentlemen. They walked rapidly towards her. Annabel flattened herself against the wall. Her heart fluttered in her throat. She tried to look as if she was waiting very definitely for someone.

One of the men raised an eyebrow as they passed her, his lips curled and his beady eyes shone out of his dusky face. She was sure he would make a cheap jibe. If they thought she was here for that kind of service so be it. She held her head high. Let them think that she was here for the pleasure of gentlemen only and that she could discern that they certainly did not qualify.

They passed her. Annabel drew in a long breath and after a moment and they were some paces ahead of her she dared to step after them. She could still hear the whistling, and wondered what these men were up to. Their pace had quickened and they turned onto *Ulica Kanonicza*, turned right, and headed after, she was sure, the whistling gentleman ripe for the picking.

Annabel quickened her step, careful not to make a sound. She reached the top of the alley and pressed herself to the right wall, still hidden. She peered around it to see what was happening in the street.

"Hey!" Mr. Champion had noticed the two men, spun around on his heels and whipped something from under his coat.

A pistol.

Annabel's breath caught. While it should be no surprise to see any gentleman armed, she prayed that he would have no occasion to use it.

The men exchanged glances and fled. Thank heavens!

Mr. Champion skidded after them. Oh, why did he not leave them alone? No good would come from chasing them.

The temperature must have dropped. The wet street was becoming icy. Annabel pulled her cloak more tightly around her.

The men turned down an alleyway to the right. They would be soon lost in a maze of small streets they probably knew like the back of their hands and their pursuer certainly would not.

There was nothing to be done except follow them, at a distance, of course. If anything happened to Mr. Champion... No, she would not consider that possibility. It made her begin to feel numb.

She walked quickly. She turned the street where he had run after the men.

And nearly walked into Mr. Champion.

She pulled herself back in time.

He had stopped and was staring, his back to her, down the street. That he'd decided not to pursue the chase any further was a good thing.

He put his pistol away.

Then he turned abruptly, before she had a chance to hide back behind the corner of the wall, and saw her.

Annabel took a deep breath and decided she would play the crone. She pulled down her hood so it obscured most of her face and stepped out into the street careful to remain in the darkest shadows. She waved her hand so he could be in no doubt of the direction to go and spoke croakily in Polish.

But he didn't turn back the way she had indicated, back up the street towards the *Collegium Juridicum*. Instead he started walking towards her.

Annabel grabbed her skirts and started to run, paying no heed to anything but the need to get away. She headed straight down the alley on her right, hearing the clatter of her boots ringing out through the empty air and making her flight impossible not to notice. *Too late now.*

The alley led nowhere but to a large wooden gate. She flung herself against it, pushing. She drew in ragged breaths and pushed harder. Nothing, the gate stood fast.

There was a round iron handle. She grasped it with both hands and tried to twist it. It wouldn't move.

She kept her head turned away, facing the gate even though she knew the footsteps had come to a halt and he was standing just behind her. She said something inconsequential in Polish she hoped would sound entirely baffling to his ears.

"Countess Szalynski?"

Annabel let her hand drop away from the handle, turned around. It was no good trying to pretend.

He dragged his fingers across his chin and blinked.

He blinked again.

She saw the vapor from her breath pollute the

air in front of her.

He blinked again, watching her.

"How did you guess?" Annabel said unable to tear her gaze away. His eyes were like coals in the dim cloudy moonlight.

"I recognized you... your figure. The way you moved. It is quite, er...unique." His face was only an arm's length from hers and each bat of his eyelashes was causing her heart to beat unevenly.

Foolish, foolish Annabel, she thought to herself and wished she could look away.

"Countess," he continued and his brow creased, "what on earth are you doing...in the street...dressed in...in that cloak, quite alone, and so late at night?"

"That is none of your concern."

"Very well." He raised an eyebrow and offered her his arm. "May I escort you home?"

"No, thank you, Mr. Champion. I am not on my way home."

"Ah. May I therefore be of service by escorting you to your destination?"

"No, thank you. There is no need." Annabel breathed deeply. She had not lied. Her destination, Zakonski's house, was only yards away, back around the corner.

"I see." He pulled his shoulders back and glanced casually about him as if this was not some dark alley but perhaps a Viennese ballroom. "You should be aware that before I left England, your uncle made it clear to me that once I arrived here I was to take you into my protection. Forgive me but I cannot conceive how it is safe for you to be out here alone at night in the city streets. Therefore—"

"I am quite safe." Annabel raised her chin high. Her eyes were nearly level with his lips. She would not let that distract her. "I know this city. It was you who were in potential danger. Those men, whoever they were—"

"I take it then that you are on your way to a...a rendezvous?" His eyebrows rose. "The anonymity, the cloak—"

"No! It's not what you think!"

There was a moment's pause. A moment when Annabel could see he was mulling over which words he should say next. He rocked backwards on his heels.

A flicker passed across his eyes. Impatience? Annoyance? "I am surprised, but I shall take you at your word, Countess," he said.

"Thank you, and I..." She let her voice trail away into the cold air. She had no choice. "I would be delighted to be taken into your protection, Mr. Champion. But you must believe me that we must talk properly first, before you do anything or anything about our association becomes public knowledge. For now it must be that we are seen to be mere acquaintances."

"Let us talk then. I understand there are some difficulties with your late husband's—?"

"No!" She drew in a breath so sharp it stung the inside of her chest. "We cannot talk here. Tomorrow perhaps. I shall try and arrange something. I will send you a note."

He looked as if he was debating whether to trust her.

"You must trust me," she said.

His expression did not change. His jaw stayed completely still. Locked. She wondered if he was thinking back to the past, when, it might be said that she'd betrayed him.

A snowflake fluttered down from the heavens. Annabel watched it land softly on his left shoulder. A tiny fleck of white against the black just for a moment before it melted.

A couple more snowflakes spun slowly downwards past her line of vision. One landed on her cheek but she hardly felt it. Annabel glanced upwards towards the sky. The moon was still strong. Not enough clouds for substantial snowfall tonight. But perhaps tomorrow...

The warm leather of his gloves cupped her chin, brushed against her cheeks, pulled her ever so slightly towards him, but he pulled himself up to her even faster.

The heat from his body hit her hard. Annabel stumbled backwards. She recognized that beyond the physical warmth was another heat even more potent—his desire.

She wondered, if she lost her footing, whether she would fall, yet knew it wouldn't happen. If she lost her balance he would catch her. She wouldn't run away, she was caught already, and was a willing prisoner.

He sealed what she knew and captured her lips with his own.

The flood of heat that enveloped her forced her eyes shut. The sudden white flame had blanketed her vision letting her other senses drink him in.

She drank. Tasted him. Juniper berries and wine and something more that was sweet and could only be him. His gloves moved upwards, pushing, towards the line of her hair and then trailed downwards into the hood of her cloak, his fingers teasing the sinews behind her ears and around the back of her neck.

Pulled even deeper into him, Annabel inhaled the scents of soap, sandalwood and ticklish pepper? And smoke from an evening spent in a room whose chimney had not been cleaned adequately and where the gentlemen had smoked cigarillos.

She couldn't think of a kiss that had ever been like this, or that a kiss could be like this.

She held on to the lapels of his cloak, dared to stroke the thick fabric with her thumbs. She didn't dare to move her hands anywhere else.

She would have liked not to have been wearing gloves. To have been able to brush his cheek, feel the touch of his skin against her own.

So vivid was this sensation, she did not even recall that they were outside, in the middle of the street, in the middle of the night...until he pulled away.

Annabel's eyes flew open, startled at the sudden rush of cold against her face.

He held his right hand clasped to his neck, was rubbing it. "This is madness! Utter madness!" He seemed to mutter to himself.

He smoothed his hand across his temples. Were they throbbing too? As hers were?

He caught her glance. Too quickly. Dropped it.

"I..." he began. Didn't finish. Frowned. He stared into the distance as if nothing was any longer satisfactory, shifting the weight between his feet.

"I should be sorry," he said in a rushed breath. "But I am not."

Not sorry? Her first thought was that he had felt it too? What she felt, she'd never felt like that before. She couldn't even think of a word for it.

Annabel's jaw stiffened, her blood was leaving her head, flowing somewhere so that she was left cold. She let her eyelids flicker shut, as if not seeing the fire would douse it.

"Countess?" His hands seized her shoulders. Did he think her so utterly foolish that she would faint?

Annabel gulped, pinned his gaze.

"What do you think you are doing?" she heard herself say in a tone as threatening as a newly sharpened knife. "How dare you...kiss me. I am not some...lady of the night."

"I should not have taken that liberty." He relaxed his grip. "Please accept my apologizes, Countess."

"I accept them. Now please let me go." She shook herself free of him and pushed her shoulders back so she could face him straighter. Her hood fell back but she let it be. She decided she could not afford to fall out with him, even if he had taken a grievous liberty.

"Annabel, my name is Annabel," she said and thought that the grievous liberty had not been unpleasant, not at all. If he was attracted to her perhaps she could use it to her advantage.

"If it pleases you, I will call you Annabel. And you may call me Henry then. Why not?" Hell, he babbled like an over-excited schoolboy. And he was forgetting she hadn't yet told him what she was doing out here, even if she spoke the truth about not knowing the two men.

"Henry."

The way she spoke it was like a curl of wood from a carpenter's lathe. It hung there for a moment, fresh in the air and then fell away. He wanted to hear it again. A thousand times from her lips would not be enough.

"Henry."

Another curl, rounded a bit differently and with an air of satisfied certainty stuck to the end of it he did not like. What sort of trickery was this? She could play a man, he had no doubt, like the finest musician might play a violin.

And yet despite it all, despite knowing the worst a woman could do, he wanted her. Henry shook himself.

"I must go." She turned and side stepped around him.

"No you don't." He seized her arm, a bit more roughly than he would have liked and pulled her against him. His first instinct was to kiss her again but he ruthlessly suppressed it.

She struggled.

"What are you doing out here?" he demanded. His voice came out like a growl. He was as angry with himself as with her. "Why are your face and clothes so dirty?"

He wanted her, not just to slate a lust, all of her and for always. A force so violent it hit hard against his chest demanding, demanding, and the kiss had only added to its strength.

There was a shout and another black-cloaked woman was running towards them. She had no hesitation on pummeling her fists hard down on his back.

"What the devil—"

"Let me go!" Annabel shouted and managed to wrest herself from his grasp as he turned to try and shake off his attacker.

The two women fled into the night.

Henry forced his feet to stay rooted exactly where they were. He wasn't going to chase them. He knew where she lived. Tomorrow would be soon enough.

He started to walk, found he was shaking.

He had been invaded. He wanted to rip it out, whatever it was, and cast it down on the ground to die. He bristled at being suddenly ruled by an ever-growing emotion he did not recognize, did not want and did not know how to control.

****

It wasn't until they reached *Ulica Szpitalna* that Annabel dared to slow down, turn around to see. He wasn't following. She didn't think he'd given chase but they had hurtled through the streets with only one thought: to escape.

Now it was just a matter of stealing back into her own house. Annabel slid under a neighbor's portico—a neighbor who was out of town—to wait while Helena checked if the coast was clear. She put a hand upon her chest, could feel the thump of her heart. Her head pounded and she was gasping, could hardly breathe. What if they had been seen? Two women running through the center of the city was not a sight so common not to be noticed. Surely no one would recognize her?

Unless they had been followed. Annabel gulped.

Ulica Szpitalna was deserted. But that was no guarantee of anything.

Why...*why* had she let him kiss her? A man she had met on so few occasions she could count them on the finger of one hand. A man who was of extreme importance to her. Oh, she was attracted to him. She knew that. And it was an attraction more powerful than any she had ever before experienced. But surely it could not be so great as to blind her to the reality of what was at stake here.

Was it a bad thing at all, if that was what he wanted? Could a stolen kiss here or there better seal the favor she wanted to ask him?

An icy rush of wind made her pull her cloak more stoutly about her, huddle in more closely to the wall. What of her own feelings on the matter?

She clenched her teeth together. No, her feelings had no bearing on the matter. The task in hand came first.

A low whistle. Annabel started and looked up. Helena stood at her back gate, beckoning.

Annabel skipped down the portico steps and hastened across the street.

What a luxury it was to be back in the safety of her own house, her own chamber. Annabel removed her cloak. Helena took it out of her hands, went and hung it up, then told Annabel to sit down.

She sat on the side of her bed. She'd gotten her breath back now but it was a welcome instruction. "Quickly," she said to Helena, "what did you learn?"

"Not good news," Helena said and her expression matched her words. "You could not have gotten in the house unseen. There is no way to get upstairs except to go through a wide atrium. With the card party going on, many of the guests were using the atrium for conversations."

"We have wasted our time."

"However, I did learn that the count does use a room as a study," Helena continued, shutting the wardrobe door. She walked over to face Annabel. "There is a desk there with a locked drawer and the room is usually locked. This I learned from my cousin. I also learned that most of the servants came with the count from his country estate. Only a very few have been hired in Krakow."

Annabel knew exactly what Helena was saying, that such servants would probably be impossible to bribe and it would be dangerous to try.

"Then we are at a dead end," Annabel said. "Unless—"

"No, you are not going back to wait alone in the street at night. You were being attacked!"

"Ah, yes, but I did know that gentleman. He wasn't attacking me. He just wanted to know what I was doing in the street, and I wouldn't tell him so he wouldn't let me go."

The frown on Helena's face had not shifted.

"He wanted to walk me home. He is a gentleman—"

"If you say it." Helena shrugged her shoulders.

"What should I do?"

"About Zakonski? Or about the gentleman who wanted to walk you home?"

"Helena!"

"I know you many years and so I say it. And I say this again. If you had remarried you would not be in this situation. Your new husband would have sorted the count out, preferably killed him."

Annabel opened her mouth to protest.

"No!" Helena waved a finger at her. "Do not

defend that animal. I know and you know it is only what he deserves. He killed Szalynski, and in cold blood. Another duel to right the wrongs of the first one."

"Another duel? Never." Annabel shuddered. "You don't know what you are talking about!" Never, ever would such a thing take place if she had anything to do with it. If she married, and she had no plans to marry, it must be to a man who would take the slur to her honor without demanding satisfaction. Zakonski had not fought fair the first time. Why would he feel obliged to play by the rules on a second outing?

"You have had plenty willing to be suitors," Helena goaded. "Let me see, there was—"

"Leave it!" Annabel snapped, hearing the anger in her own voice.

"You are tired." Helena's countenance softened. "Go to bed now."

"Yes." She was too tired to think. She did not want to think.

Chapter Eight

A banging of doors and shouting. Henry's eyes flew open as he struggled into consciousness. It was dark, still the middle of the night and all he could see in front of him was velvet blackness. What the hell was going on?

Had thieves broken into the house?

He was lying in a tangle of bedclothes and it took a moment to get himself out. Too long, Henry thought, ignoring the thumping of blood in his head that demanded he lay it down again on his pillow.

He ripped back the counterpane, grabbed his pistol and pouch from behind the bolster and leapt out of bed. His feet landed on the woolen rug next to his bed almost noiselessly just as he had practiced so many times.

He padded to the door of his chamber, turned the handle slowly. He could hear someone, no, several people, coming up the stairs. It sounded as if they carried something heavy.

And someone groaned loudly. Had someone been injured in a fight?

The odds were that this was some commotion caused by the servants. Henry debated for a moment whether or not to load his pistol. There appeared to be too many people involved for this to be house breakers. It must be the servants.

But doing what? He edged his door open slowly, enough to peer around.

He saw Marek draped across the shoulders of two footmen reaching the top of the stairs. Marek had a bloodshot eye and blood trickling down the side of his face. They were followed by more servants.

Marek was injured and it looked nasty. What on earth had happened?

Henry tossed his pistol on the bed, and decided to ignore the fact that he was dressed only in a nightgown and that his bare legs would be proposed by the housemaids as the talk of the servant's hall tomorrow. Let them talk. Marek looked in a bad way.

Henry stepped into the hallway, shutting his door behind him.

"Marek? What on earth—"

"Alive...I'm alive," Marek croaked. A maid with a sponge pushed forward and dabbed at the blood on Marek's face.

"Never had you down as a great pugilist. It was supposed to be a card evening. What the hell happened?"

"Footpads." Marek managed a weak smile before his eyelids shuttered and his face contorted with pain.

Henry ran his hand through his hair.

Pan Jacob, one of the senior servants, who had been following the procession with a taper, stepped forward. He said to him in German that all was in hand and that they were putting Marek to bed.

"Sir? What is going on? Anything I can do?"

Robards had appeared at last.

"Yes, go with that lot and see that Count Ralenski is being looked after properly. I am sure they know what they are doing, but... And see if you can find out what happened."

"Right-ho, sir." Robards checked the fastening of his dressing gown and then sped off after the train that was disappearing down the corridor.

There was nothing he could do now except go back to bed Henry decided. But that footpads had

attacked Marek worried him. Could he really have
been a random victim of robbery?

****

"Come in!" Marek's voice barked.

Henry pushed the door fully open and stepped
into Ralenski's chamber. It took him a moment to
adjust his gaze. Despite the shutters being drawn,
the morning sun filtered in through small slits but it
wasn't enough to dispel the deliberate dimness.

"Ah, Henry. Good morning." Marek sat in his
bed, propped up by carefully arranged pillows. A
tray with coffee had been placed on a low table
beside him. The coffee cup was full, untouched. The
skin around Marek's left eye was tinged yellow. It
would be black by tomorrow Henry thought.

"How are you feeling?" he asked.

"Not very good. And not just from that vile
Muscovite champagne Zakonski was serving, the
cheapskate. As you can see." Marek groaned and
moved his hand an inch so he could hold the cold
compress on a different angle of his forehead. "You
know I tell you one day not to wander about the city
at night because of footpads. Then I go and get
attacked myself!"

"What happened?" Henry walked over to the far
corner of the room and picked up a wooden chair. He
placed it beside the bed and sat down.

"They set on me just after I had left Zakonski's,"
Marek said with a grimace. "I should have come
with you earlier, but I was on such a good run. The
card table is only supposed to hurt my pocket, not
my whole body!"

"What was the motive? Robbery?"

"Of course! They got the money I had on me. But
I did send them packing before they did too much
damage to me. Ha! There were only two of them and
I have been a hussar. If only I had had time to draw
my sword I would have given them a proper lesson."

"Two men, you say? What did they look like?"

"One tall, one short and burley. Why do you ask? Did you see any fellows lurking on your way home?" Could it be the same footpads who had set on him, Henry wondered. The same men he had chased away last night? And when the footpads had accosted him on his way to Annabel's house that first time could it have been Marek they were waiting for? Henry was aware of another suspicion forming in his mind.

"And was there a woman with them at all?" Exactly what had Annabel been doing outside Zakonski's house disguised in a filthy cloak? She hadn't said, nor had she wanted to be recognized initially, of that he was certain.

"A woman? No."

"Are you sure you didn't see a woman lingering about?" Henry pressed.

"No, that I would remember." Marek frowned and looked thoughtful.

Henry tried to make sense of the many thoughts that were running through his mind. There seemed to be two key questions. Was Annabel in league with Zakonski and was Marek in danger?

"No, no woman," Marek said with an air of finality. "I might have had rather too much of that filthy champagne but I was wide awake the moment they set on me."

"It might have been the same footpads who accosted me," Henry said. "From your description."

"Really?" Marek frowned and started to push himself upwards. His face contorted with pain and he slumped back down defeated.

"You know, Henry," he said after a pause, "there are some things going on here I don't quite understand but there is a possibility it was not robbery. That our friends the footpads have a leader, a higher motive. There are people here in Krakow who would be happy to see the back of me."

"I understand," Henry replied. He didn't understand the ins and outs of it but Marek had vociferously supported Napoleon and Polish independence. In the new climate of a defeated Poland he could be classed as dangerous, by the Austrians, or the Russians.

"We have a magnificent party to go to next week," Marek said. "And I shall be better by then and we shall go for you must see hospitality in true Polish style. But after that, I may not linger in Krakow long. I'm sorry, Henry, I know you wanted to see more of Poland but perhaps it won't be possible."

"Of course. Not if things are dangerous."

"Anyway, this will be a damn good party. Count Berekowski writes an invitation to the betrothal of his daughter, Ewa, which takes place at Castle Szalynski. Everyone will be there. And of course the Countess Szalynski, Henry. Are you listening, friend?"

Of course he had been listening. It was at the mention of Annabel he'd turned his face away so that Marek would not see his reaction to the news.

Not only was his interest in Annabel developing into something so compelling he could hardly control it, but there was every probability that she was a danger to his friend. Well, he would seduce her, in that case. He would play her at her own game. And then he would strike, and find out exactly what she was up to before he carted her back to England.

"Yes. I think I shall visit the countess today."

"No you won't. It's Sunday, my friend, and the countess will be doing what all good people do on Sunday, going to church."

"Which church?"

Marek's brow creased with disapproval.

"Which church?" Henry repeated.

"*Kosciol Mariacki* I would wager would be most

likely. St. Mary's Basilica, beside the main market square. You will have walked past it several times already. Vast and gothic, you won't miss it."
****

She must pray that Count Aleksander finish his business in Russia and come to Krakow as soon as possible, for the Berekowski betrothal party at the castle if not before. She must pray for herself, and for all her servants and those who depended on her, especially Helena—

The organ music veered into a new swirl. Behind it Annabel heard the brief swish of robes, the priests and attendants gathering for their entry procession, before this was lost in a cacophony of scraping and shuffling as the congregation rose to stand.

Annabel flickered her eyes open, snapped her small prayer book shut and rose to her feet. Helena sitting beside her did likewise, acting as much as her companion as her maid. There would be other of her servants here, she knew, who mostly sat towards the back.

As was her habit, and the habit of many, she glanced backwards to watch the procession coming down the shiny floor of the nave towards her. The church was now full and the people sat around her she recognized even if they were not gentry and she knew not their names.

One face was familiar but not because she had seen him here before. Mr. Champion sat two rows behind her on the other side of the nave. Alone it seemed. Ralenski was not with him.

He caught her gaze, just for a moment. Annabel gasped. And then the procession glided past her, blocking her view.

There was nothing she could do but stare to the front, towards the beautiful medieval altar for the rest of the mass. She now knew that he sat behind her, and could be watching her at his leisure.

The priest had started the mass and the familiar Latin washed over her.

She should be concentrating on the liturgy, understanding it and speaking every word of the responses with heartfelt sincerity. She shouldn't be thinking about Mr. Champion and what had happened last night, and how she had felt when he kissed her.

Annabel pressed her hands together and focused her eyes on the gilded St. Mary at her coronation. She sat at the very top of the altar flanked on her left by St. Stanislaw of Krakow and on her right by St. Vojtech of Bohemia. Annabel tried to keep her mind on the mass.

She couldn't. What was he doing here? Had he come to this church specifically to see her?

She should not be so worried. Surely this was what she wanted. If he was interested in her in that way, then it would be easy to get him to help her.

But she had not thought her own heart would become involved in this scheme. She must detach it. And get him to agree to help her without delay. Every day she lingered, so did the danger.

He wasn't there when she came to file out once the mass had finished. Had he slipped away early? Annabel had no way of knowing.

Just before she and Helena reached the door a figure appeared beside her. A prickle rippled down her neck. Without looking she knew it was him.

He offered his arm and silently she placed her hand on his sleeve. A gesture that felt far more intimate to her than it by rights should. Helena had the sense to fall a step behind them.

He didn't speak until they were outside.

"Good morning, Countess Szalynski." The sharp breeze whipped his coat tails about the tops of his legs—legs she thought would look even finer astride a fine mount.

She would be blushing in a minute if she didn't push such wanton thoughts to the very back of her mind.

"Good morning, Henry," she replied, deliberately ignoring his formality. She couldn't ever think she had noticed a man's legs in such a way before. She was pleased to hear her voice sounded even. "I am surprised that Count Ralenski is not with you."

She caught his gaze. He did not smile. In fact his jaw looked as if it had been set in stone. The back of her neck prickled.

"Yes," he said. "I would speak with you on that subject."

"Oh? I am not sure I understand—"

"Perhaps. Or perhaps you know more than you are letting on." What did he think she knew? And why had his voice developed an edge to it? Like a blade being sharpened on granite. Annabel glanced about her, as usual people were milling around, catching up with neighbors before they made their way home. Yet she could be watched even now.

"Can we talk?" he said.

"Not here. I must go. We should not be seen lingering together like this."

"Oh? And why is that?" He laid his hand over hers, trapping her fingers against his sleeve. "We must talk in private? A coffee house perhaps?"

He smiled but she did not believe it. She was too close to him yet she was unable to take a step back.

"No," she said keeping her voice low. "Not a kawiarnia. I don't know where. I must think. I will send you a note."

"Today?" It was hardly a question.

"Today," she agreed.

He lifted his hand from hers but seized her fingers before she had time to remove them and pulled her gloved hand to his lips.

Annabel trembled. What if Zakonski or his spies were abroad and were watching her now? Let them see it as only the most ordinary of gestures.

He let her fingers go, couldn't hide, it seemed, his reluctance at doing so. He placed his own hands by his sides. Yes, but he needed to realize that this was not England, not just a flirtation, not a game. Maybe she could tell him the part of it if she could trust him. She did not know yet. She needed to think.

"Good day, Henry," she said with a nod.

"Good day." He lifted his hat, bowed. He turned and began walking away.

"Let's go," she said to Helena in Polish.

"So that was the gentleman from last night," Helena said. "I recognize his back. And he is English. He dresses very well. He must be rich. Marry him and go to England."

"I did not ask for your opinion."

****

It was three hours since he had left her outside the church. Henry stopped. If he kept pacing around the room as he did for much longer he would be in danger of wearing away the floor. He smiled to himself. It wasn't much of a joke but in the context of everything turning so grim... Marek was still in bed. The doctor had advised he would recover sooner if he didn't try to get up too quickly. Marek had promised he wouldn't move until tomorrow and had ordered one of the grooms, known for his skill at woodworking, to fashion him a crutch.

Henry went over to the window. He was in the front sitting room that overlooked *Ulica Florianska*. He thought he might see from here any messenger coming. The street was quiet. It was Sunday after all.

If no message came? He had that problem covered. He'd run her to ground in her own house.

Kate Allan

And he would do it tonight. It wasn't gentlemanly to break into a lady's house but if she knew who had done this to Marek he wasn't letting her escape.

Tonight, however, in hours, was still some time away.

And if she was connected with Marek's assailants that was plenty of time for her to warn them, plot, plan. Henry unclenched his fists. He was a step behind, several steps behind.

Unless it was simple robbery.

Then why had she said, *We should not be seen lingering together like this?*

An orderly tap at the door. He opened it to Robards.

"A note came for you downstairs," Robards said, holding out a letter. "You said to me you were expecting one so I brought it straight up."

"Good man." Henry took it, broke the seal with his finger and unfolded the piece of paper. He smiled as he read the letter. "Ah," he said. "A professor at the Krakow Academy, the University, interested to ask me about some matters, writes. I shall call on him today."

Henry balled the paper and threw it on the fire. If the professor was entirely fictitious and the note got into the wrong hands...

"Will you be requiring my services, sir?"

"Yes, you can come with me. Why not." Just in case it was a set up, a trap, another pair of fists might come in handy.

The *Collegium Maius* was not far. It took them only five minutes to walk there.

"The heart of the Academy, sir," Robards said as he planted a stout knock on the door. "This is the oldest part. Fourteenth century apparently."

"You have been studious yourself, Robards. Your girl been filling you in on local history?"

"Ah." Robards coughed into his cuff. "Me and her

reached an impasse."

Henry chuckled.

"So I won't need to be worrying about her father no more," Robards added.

"Ah, well, there are plenty of fish in the sea."

"Yes, and I've seen myself a nice trout I'll be after next."

"Robards, I don't know what's come over you. Since we've been here—"

"It's these Polish girls, sir. Awful friendly. Helena she's called. Trouble is, she is a servant at another house—"

"Thank heavens for that."

"So I don't know when I'll be seeing her next. Only met her today. She was in our kitchens visiting a friend of hers what is a maid at our house. And we got talking. And she speaks a bit of English—"

The large door opened and a round-faced youth, some sort of servant Henry supposed, beckoned them inside.

Henry began in German.

"Angelski?" the youth queried.

"Tak," Robards replied and the youth nodded and motioned for them to come inside.

"He asked if we were English, sir."

"Yes, I gathered that."

The youth closed the door behind them and motioned for them to follow. The entrance led straight into a medieval cloistered courtyard. They walked through a door and up some curved stone stairs to the first floor. Along a corridor they were shown into a room, a sitting room, with several chaises and a roaring fire.

The college seemed very quiet, no one about but then Henry remembered it was Sunday. He took a seat and Robards followed suit. A maid appeared after only a few minutes and set down a tray with coffee and cakes.

"This is very nice," Robards said and picked the plate up and offered it to Henry. "Would you like a piece? The poppy seed one is good. I've had it before. Who'd of thought of putting poppy seeds in a cake."

"No thanks, but don't let me stop you."

"Thank you, sir." Robards helped himself to three slices of different cakes and settled back to eat them with gusto.

Henry poured the cream from the little jug into his coffee and stirred it. He wondered for a moment whether by any chance the letter had actually been from a genuine professor.

The door opened and an elderly man who just might be a professor came in.

"Mr. Champion?" he said in flawless English. "Delighted to meet you. Come with me. Your man is very welcome to wait here. Finish the cakes, eh?"

"Thank you," Henry said, rising to shake the man's hand. "Your English is very good, professor."

"I was for a few years in Scotland. At the University in Edinburgh."

Really? Damn, Henry thought. A real professor. Not a foil by Annabel so they might meet. Her note might even now be at home waiting for him. He'd better make this visit as short as possible.

Chapter Nine

Henry walked with the professor through the college until they came to a wooden door, just like many others they had passed.

"Please, go in," the professor said opening the door. "Someone will come for you in about half an hour."

Henry stilled for a moment. He saw a flicker of confusion pass over the old man's face in response to his questioning glance and so straightened his features and went into the room as bidden.

An empty room with a desk piled with papers at one end and at the other a fire and around it some low chairs. A study or a tutorial room perhaps, Henry was not sure. There was one window, very high up the wall, and long thick curtains that reached the floor.

The door closed behind him.

Henry sneezed. It must be dusty.

"Bless you," a woman's voice said, muffled.

Henry's hand flew under his coat, clasped his pistol as he swung around. He looked around him, saw no one. He didn't think it was possible a person could be hidden in the small cupboard in the corner. The curtains? It could only be the curtains.

He leapt forward but before he even had a chance to wrest them back, the curtains moved. From behind them stepped Annabel.

"Good afternoon, Henry," she said, tucking a tendril of hair.

"I thought the professor was genuine." Henry forgot what he was doing here. His mind raced trying to find the reason. His gaze took in the shape of her face, settled on her eyelashes as they moved.

"He is genuine." She laughed. "We must talk and it must be private. We have some time. Half an hour. It cannot be longer. I do not want to raise suspicions."

She had said something like that outside the church.

"Why?" Henry couldn't hide the note of urgency in his voice.

"If I can trust you, I can tell you all of it. If not..."

"You told me last night that you trusted me."

His eyes spoke the words as much as his lips. Annabel took in a long breath. "I would like to trust you."

His gaze flickered to the ground and then caught hers again as surely as if he had seized her arms. Now was not the time to imagine being swept into his arms and into a kiss like the kiss of yesterday. Annabel shook herself. She couldn't bear his intense scrutiny any longer. She let her gaze drop and watched his shoulders. There would never be a time for such foolishness.

"Count Ralenski was set upon on his way home last night."

"Oh no!" She looked up and saw the brief flash of pain in his tight expression. "How is he?"

Was Marek alive even? Something ran through her, stealing her blood. She felt faint.

"He was set upon by two men. The same two men, I think, that I chased last night and the same two men who faced me off in an alley the night I came to your reception."

"Zakonski's men," she heard herself muttering. "The men, they may work for Zakonski."

"Are you telling me that Zakonski would like to see Count Ralenski...dead?"

"Perhaps. Or it may simply be a warning."

"A warning?"

"Yes."

"A warning about what?" His voice cracked with impatience.

"Zakonski killed my husband. You must know that. Everybody knows it."

"In a duel."

"It was murder." Annabel clasped her hands together, did not know if she could continue. Her throat was closing, tears pricking at the backs of her eyes. This was no way for her to behave. She had to remain strong.

He stepped closer. She heard his even breathing. She opened her mouth but still didn't trust herself to speak.

"Tell me why you think it could be a warning."

His timbre sounded so soft she thought she might break. Like a glass vase already weakened from a hairline crack.

"A warning not to interfere..."

Her heart skipped a beat as his ungloved finger stroked her cheek. He caught the tear and brushed it away.

"Interfere in...what?"

"There is a disagreement between the two families about some lands. You might call it a feud. It goes back a long time, before my husband was born. Both families claim that they have the right to the castle and the surrounding villages. Zakonski thought he could kill my husband and have it all his way. But I took the family papers to the magistrate and they ruled that the castle and lands should stay in the Szalynski family. However, the papers were mysteriously stolen one night from the magistrate's house. I believe that Count Zakonski has taken the papers so that we cannot prove the lands should be ours. He wants to go to court again. My husband's brother Alexsander is at last on his way back from St. Petersburg. I received a letter from him this morning and he will be here within a week or two. Then there will be another court case. In the meantime I will do everything I can to prevent Count Zakonski from taking those lands."

Annabel stopped. She was not going to explain that she had wanted to see if Zakonski had the papers and steal them back from him.

"I am not sure I understand. Why should Count Ralenski be a danger?"

"He was a good friend and confidante of my husband and he has good standing and some influence. I am certain that Count Zakonski would prefer he was absent from any court case."

"I see. So there is little we can do except wait for the return of the new Count Szalynski?"

Annabel nodded. "Yes, he has inherited the title. But I invited Count Berekowski to use the castle. Zakonski will not dare do anything with so many people there."

He looked at her directly but she fixed her gaze on the innocuous third black button of his jacket. Her heart pattered far too quickly as it was.

"May I ask you to tell me a little of your family?" she managed. "And where you live in England? I should like to hear." She glanced up.

"My family?" He raised an eyebrow but his countenance was closed. Had she asked the wrong thing? "I have one sister in England who is happily married to a very good fellow. As for the rest, it is rather a sorry tale. Perhaps your family has been more fortunate in their history?"

"Perhaps they have, but now you intrigue me." She didn't let go of his gaze. She didn't want to talk about her family. She wanted to know about his.

"As you wish," he conceded. She was not certain he looked entirely happy about telling her. "My parents both died of the Scarlet Fever."

"I am sorry," Annabel said quietly.

"Not as much as I. I was only a boy at the time." His eyes flickered and she could only guess at the confused mass of emotions that might lie hidden behind. He fingered his chin, an uncharacteristic gesture that sat ill against the poise he had cultivated hitherto.

A wave of compassion ran through her, quite violently. Annabel was seized by the urge that she should comfort him, as if he was still a small boy. She wanted to hold him in her arms. She felt a strange sense of bonding with him. He would know what it felt like to lose your parents. Perhaps he had felt as she had. No, he could not have felt as she had, for unlike her, he'd not been responsible for his parents' deaths.

"Oh dear," she said and knew she must sound confused. It was hardly the thing to say but he struck at her every sense, quite effortlessly. Annabel breathed deeply.

"My father was a Naturalist. We had gone to the West Indies on one of his expeditions." He spoke softly, deliberately, so that she had the impression that he was telling her something about himself very real. As if she had by chance kicked a stone away and found a pearl underneath. "He caught something out there. Not the Scarlet Fever, that came later when we were back in England, but something that weakened him in the chest. He found it difficult to work after that and my mother found it difficult to manage everything. We were lucky, my sister and I, for she had sent us on an extended stay to our aunt. We were not at home when they were taken sick."

"Perhaps you have inherited an appetite for travel from your father? Do you have an interest too in flora and fauna?"

"No," he said. "I find people a lot more interesting."

Did he find her *interesting*? "People are very interesting," she agreed. "How did you come to meet Count Ralenski?"

"In Paris."

"How delightful." Now, quickly she must think of something to say next...

"Annabel, might I be permitted to inquire a little into your history?"

"My history?" Annabel feigned an expression of astonishment and cast her gaze up towards the ceiling. She could laugh this off. She was well practiced at that. She smiled, knew it was a vacuous, forced smile, and hoped nevertheless he was taken in.

"You know surely that I am the daughter of the late Lord and Lady Wells?" Did he really not remember her? Not remember that time they met in such scandalous circumstances at the Farringham's ball? "I married my husband, Count Szalynski, very young. I came to Poland as a consequence of my marriage. My husband was killed." She looked at him. "There is little else of consequence to tell."

"I should like to hear it."

She tried to fix her face in a haughty expression, fight back at his unrepentant appraisal. His eyes were doing it now, taking in every inch of her, unashamedly. "Mr. Champion," she said before she could help herself, "why do you look at me so? You watch me all the time."

"Because I find you... Fascinating."

Annabel tried to interest herself in the pattern on the curtains—without much success. Had she really heard him correctly?

"Annabel, do you...remember that we knew each other before? Before you got married, back in England?"

"Yes," Annabel whispered. Her eyes seemed to have decided they were fascinated by the way his chest heaved and fell as he breathed. She lifted her gaze and caught his. A tremor radiated through her body to every corner, and then a second. She couldn't for the moment think what to say. She couldn't think of anything except that she wanted him to touch her, to kiss her.

"I will not deny that I find you an attractive woman. Then, as now." Henry's body seemed to stiffen. He pulled at his collar. "I will control myself. You are in my protection and although you are a widow, it would be utterly reprehensible for me to overstep the mark. I overstepped the mark last night. I ask for your forgiveness. I had drunk a quantity of brandy."

There was a rap on the door.

Annabel gulped. If he was going to say it he had better say it quickly. "I had rather hoped... Hoped that..."

Henry appeared to pale. She bit her lip. "Hope that we might..."

"I have no interest in empty flirtation." His voice sounded like a cold, wooden board. He might as well have slapped her in the face.

"Forgive me," she muttered, and turned so that she no longer had to look at him. What he must think of her, she could only too well conceive. "Perhaps you should go."

Whoever was at the door knocked again.

"But..." His tone softened. "That we should become friends, that I should like. After all, we must trust one another and then we must travel together back to England."

She did not want to hear it. Nothing he said now could plaster over the cracks that had occurred between them. Nothing she said could take them back to where they had gotten to before she so foolishly spoke. She turned back, although she did not look at him, and bid whoever was at the door to enter.

It was the round-faced youth.

"You had better go," she said.

Henry lifted her bare fingers to his lips. He kissed them. His touch still made her quiver. Yet, all she wanted at this moment was to be rid of him so that she could nurse her hurt alone.

"*Au revior*," he said. "Until we meet again."

"I trust it will be soon," she replied unsure whether or not she meant it.

****

"A noble sentiment," Marek said, pulling his horse at the bit to turn the animal around, "to offer to escort Countess Szalynski. But does she need escorting? Has the Count not returned? I find it remarkable that you appear to have developed so close an acquaintance with the countess in such a short time. Is there something you are not telling me, dear friend?"

They were in the courtyard at the back of Marek's house preparing to leave for Castle Szalynski. The castle was five or six hours ride away and they had elected to ride horses. A carriage with the servants and baggage would follow. Annabel had written him a note to say that her brother-in-law had returned from St. Petersburg. He intended to stay in Krakow overnight before proceeding directly to the castle where he intended to throw a grand homecoming party to coincide with the party already planned to celebrate the Berekowski betrothal. Henry assumed the count must have left for the castle already or Marek was right that she would need no escort. There was to be much gaiety and fine company at Castle Szalynski in the coming days but that is not what gladdened Henry's heart. Rather that now Count Szalynski had returned there was nothing standing in the way of them returning to England.

Henry had, of course, at once offered to escort her to the castle. He'd not seen her for three weeks, though they shared the same city, and he found he felt excited and somewhat elated at the prospect that he would see her again, within minutes.

"Nothing more than the fact that the countess is a fellow countryman," Henry lied, realizing that Marek still waited for an answer from him. He put his foot into the stirrup and mounted. He gave the chestnut mare a pat on her flank. He did not like to lie to Marek but he hadn't told him that he and Annabel were previously acquainted, or that he intended to accompany her back to England. "I assumed you would have no objection. I am sorry if—"

"No objection as such. Merely an observation. And it is this. That one who puts his hand in the fire is liable to get burned."

Henry gritted his teeth and stopped himself retorting unwisely. He had not said anything yet to Marek about Annabel's suspicions that his attackers may have been connected to Count Zakonski. Marek seemed determined that it was simple robbery. So determined, in fact, that Henry was sure Marek knew better than he the motive of his assailants.

"There is more going on here than you may see, Henry," Marek continued in a quieter voice. "Be wary."

They trotted out of the back gate and up into *Ulica Florianska*.

"What exactly are you telling me?" Henry ventured. There was no doubt now in Henry's mind. Marek knew.

"I am not telling you anything in a public street," Marek said and grinned. A group of three smartly dressed women who had been walking down the street stopped to observe them. Marek waved at them and they shyly acknowledged him with their eyes. "We cut quite a dash I think."

Henry could not help smiling. He flicked his reins and they trotted side by side up to the top of the street and through the gate in the city walls and to the Barbican where they were to meet Annabel.

Her carriage was there, waiting in front of the red brick redoubt, beside a lady mounted astride a large black stallion. She trotted up to them.

It was Annabel, dressed in a burgundy colored riding habit with a matching cap dressed with ivory and pink feathers. He had not seen her since a rather crowded reception they had attended. Henry regarded her every tuck and curve from head to toe. It fitted her slender form perfectly.

"Good morning," she called. "Henry, you look like a fish. Have you never seen a lady astride a horse before?"

Henry pressed his lips together. Perhaps he had been gaping. He shifted his boots in his stirrups.

"Countess, do not tease poor Henry so," Marek said. "You of all people know in England the custom is different and that there ladies ride side saddle."

"Good morning, Countess." Henry kept his tone light. "I was startled to see what a fine figure you present mounted. I had not expected to see you riding. And your stallion too. Magnificent. Is he Arabian?"

"His father was pure Arab but not his mother."

"Where is Szalynski?" Marek called out. "Has he been delayed?"

"No, he returned to Krakow three days ago but decided yesterday to go straight on to the castle." She smiled. "It is chiefly his home, you know."

"You are an excellent caretaker of Castle Szalynski, I have no doubt," Market replied. "And the fine idea of inviting Count Berekowski to celebrate his daughter's betrothal there was yours?"

"It was. Thank you."

Henry thought he saw a slight blush on her cheeks.

"Shall we go?" Marek kicked his steed into action.

The road out of the city was wide and they rode three abreast for quite a while.

"I am curious, Mr. Champion," Annabel said. She called him by his proper appellation in public. "What made you join the army?"

"I had a small estate near Sevenoaks in Kent, a day's ride from London, which I inherited. I tried to play the country squire but I was young and restless. I could afford a modest commission so joined the army. I went with my regiment to the Iberian Peninsula, ended up as an aide-de-camp to the colonel."

"And you, Ralenski?"

"Much simpler. I fancied myself as a dashing Hussar," Marek replied. "The dress is splendid. Quite unsurpassed. On this matter I find all ladies agree."

Henry couldn't help smiling.

"We are fortunate the weather is so clement today." Marek lifted his chin slightly and took in a long breath of air.

"I was worried it might snow it has been so cold these past weeks," Annabel replied. "Really it should not be snowing in April, but sometimes it can happen."

Henry remembered the snowflakes that night he had kissed her. He pushed the unwelcome memory to the back of his mind.

Chapter Ten

"Have you met the Duke of Wellington, Mr. Champion?" she asked him a little later when their horses slowed again to trot.

"Frequently. I served for a short time as one of his aides and then was with him in Vienna."

"You are very clever of course," she said. "Wellington must have seen that."

"Nothing compared to the great man himself. You flatter me." In fact he had the distinct impression she was being flirtatious with him.

"Each man has an opportunity to be great in some sphere. It is a woman's misfortune not to have been born a man." She spoke with confidence but there was something downcast in her voice. "A woman might shine in her own home. That is all, I think."

"Unless she is a queen, or a lover of kings," Marek said. "Then she might wield a great deal of influence."

Henry wanted to say something meaningful, partly to mitigate Marek's playfulness, partly because he wanted to give Annabel something she could see to be true that was for a woman beyond the confines of home and family. He could not think what to say. It was true that women were confined to their own spheres. That was the natural order of things.

"Do you mean a frightening amount of influence?" she teased Marek.

Marek looked unconcerned.

Then it came to Henry that he should tell her

about his mother. "My mother helped my father a great deal in his work as a Naturalist. She was very good and did much of his drawing. She also wrote up from his notes and helped keep his notes in order. He would not have managed half of what he did without her."

"Yes, a woman may be a Naturalist so long as her husband is also and she can publish using his name."

"Is it not enough to be a rich and beautiful, Countess?" Marek interrupted.

"No, it is not enough." Annabel smiled. "But I have started several schools for the village children. I have not been completely idle."

They stopped after a couple of hours to give the horses water. Annabel's maid served a delicious picnic of cold sausage and pickled cucumbers. They ate their meal in the comfort of Annabel's carriage which was grander and more spacious than Marek's.

"Here we are, sir," the maid said to Henry as she handed him a plate. Henry was surprised to hear English being spoken by a servant.

Later, as he returned from having walked a little way down the road to stretch his legs before they set off again, Henry noticed Robards smiling amiably at her and indulging in some light banter as she cleared the things away. Could this be the English-speaking maid that Robards had said he had his eye on?

What a possible stroke of luck if it was! Henry pulled out his handkerchief and sneezed to hide his smile. Hurrah for Robards. Such an association could prove a useful source of intelligence indeed.

After another two hours in the saddle, Henry concluded that tomorrow might prove to be a little painful. They had turned off the main road some time ago and were trotting single file onto what was little more than a track, though it was wide enough for carriages. The hard, uneven ground was going to leave them frightfully saddle-sore.

Again he was jolted into the air and landed back down with a thump. Henry gritted his teeth. It was starting to hurt but perhaps it wasn't as uncomfortable as traveling the same road in a carriage. Besides, they had left the carriages some way behind. One advantage of horseback was that they would reach their destination quicker.

"Ah-ha!" Marek shouted and drew his mount up to Henry's side as they slowed. "See there? The village ahead? And the hill to the left? You can't see the castle from here but it's there, perched on the other side of that hill."

Henry cast his eye across the green plain, took in the small village nestled at the base of the sudden hill. From the top of that hill you would, from this side at least, have a view for miles. It made sense why the castle was perched on the other side of the hill. The side that faced them was mostly a sheer drop where not even bushes grew.

"Now are we too tired," Marek said, "or do we canter the final bit?"

"We canter," Annabel said with a smile and flicked her ribbons.

Henry gave it everything he had and yet neither he nor Marek caught up with her.

They rode through the village and then the ground began to incline steeply. Henry's mare, he quickly learned to his relief, knew what she was doing.

They dismounted at the foot of the hill where the stabling and outbuildings were and walked the final hundred yards up to the castle gates.

A groom was already leading Annabel's stallion away and she stood, her cheeks flushed crimson and her eyes sparking.

"What took you both so long?" She laughed.

Henry felt something in his chest crumple. This Annabel, who could ride a horse as fierce as the devil for nearly five hours and still be smiling, he wanted as his own.

They would have five daughters, each one unique and yet each one just like her.

Henry slid out of his saddle and onto the firm ground. He needed a stiff drink. Vodka.

He was a fool and he deserved to suffer for it. She'd never marry him.

Henry kicked a stone out of his way. It was inconceivable that a gentleman engaged in work such as he could be a suitable husband. It was hardly an occupation of honor. He had sworn an oath to the Crown and that came above gentlemanly honor, truth and friendship. Would that he were in England, engaged in no occupation aside from the maintenance of his estates, arriving at a house party. And that she was a debutante of average standing, who would be over the moon at a proposal from a single gentleman regarded as a minor hero of Waterloo, and with a comfortable income.

A different stage with different players, he mused, and looked up. While he'd stared at the ground like a sullen schoolboy she had taken Marek's arm and they had started walking up towards the castle. Henry quickened his step and caught them up. He followed behind as they went inside the gates, designed originally to keep people out, and through the grim stonework. They emerged into a wide courtyard overlooked on three sides by four stories of open balconies, like suspended cloisters.

Two finely-dressed ladies were promenading the third storey balcony, and they stopped and waved.

Marek waved back enthusiastically. He turned to Henry. "The tall one with the dark hair, that is Countess Gronowski if I'm not mistaken. With luck her husband will be here because he's a fine fellow. And the younger lady is Countess Mielszenski. I see already we are going to have some enjoying of ourselves to do!"

A heavy door slammed and a tall, imposing man swept into the courtyard to greet them. Count Szalynski never paused a moment from laughing.

Henry stood and smiled, and nodded when it seemed appropriate. A few words were exchanged in French but Szalynski spoke the rest of the time extremely fast and in Polish before servants appeared to show them to their chambers. Szalynski appeared no fool, and Henry wondered how similar he was to his late elder brother. And whether his arrival meant that Annabel would now be happy to come back to England.

****

Robards was perfecting the knot of Henry's cravat when there was a knock at the door and Marek entered.

"You English with your fancy neckcloths," Marek drawled. "You always take so long to dress!"

"I wouldn't want to let the side down," Henry replied, trying not to move his mouth much in case it disturbed his valet at the critical moment.

"You know, Henry," Marek said, resting his hand on the back of a chair and leaning on it, "I'm not sure how long I am going to stay here."

"What? Here at the castle?"

"No, in Poland; not that there is such a thing as Poland anymore. I thought I should tell you maybe your visit might have to be a bit shorter than you planned. I'm sorry."

"What are your plans?" He hoped Marek did not intend to leave immediately. It might be very difficult for him to stay on here with his host, and when he left, he was taking Annabel with him.

"I might lease the house out to someone who

wants to live there, but I'm not sure I do. Krakow is supposed to be a free city. Ha! That makes me laugh. A clause in a treaty to keep the balance of power in Europe balanced, nothing more. Tell me, if the Austrians marched into Krakow tomorrow and took the place with force what would anyone do? Would the British come and assist?"

"No," Henry replied after a moment's pause. "Not now that Napoleon has been vanquished. It was difficult enough for Lord Liverpool when he was Prime Minister to get Parliament to support pushing forward the campaign in the Peninsula beyond preserving Portuguese interests by defending the Torres Verdes. It was, perhaps, only the renewed threat of an invasion of our own shores that swung it for Wellington to get the supplies he needed."

"Europe doesn't need another war." Marek shook his head although he kept his eyes fixed straight ahead. "Everyone wants peace. The cause of Polish independence is doomed for a generation at least."

"There we are." Robards flicked what was probably an invisible speck of dust off his handiwork. "All done, sir."

Henry wanted to say something along the lines that hope should not be abandoned but the Vienna treaty had been signed by the powers of Europe. Nothing short of a bloody revolution would free Poland of Russian suzerainty now. And just the word *revolution* was enough to make a sane man shudder. Look what the revolution had led to in France.

"I might go back to Paris," Marek said. "Or London."

"Come to England." Henry wondered if the attack from the footpads had precipitated Marek's decision. "You'd be welcome as my guest for as long as you like, as you know."

"Thank you, Henry." Marek slapped him on the back. "But before we go anywhere we have much enjoying of ourselves to do and in the Polish style!"

****

"Oh, no, please allow me to serve you with this most tender looking cut." Marek stabbed a fork elegantly into the plate of meat proffered by the footman and flirted outrageously with the young lady who sat between them at dinner. Countess Mielszenski spoke English remarkably well and unnerved Henry by looking at him with her long eyelashes all a-quiver.

"Where did you two blades meet?" she asked.

"We met in Paris, didn't we, Henry?" Marek replied.

"Yes. Paris."

Around sixty guests were dining in the great hall. The high walls were lined with Flemish tapestries, perhaps to help dampen the noise from the chatter and clatter of cutlery that rose mercilessly like flames licking their way up a tall bonfire.

Still there were spare places as yet unoccupied, waiting for late arrivals. Henry noticed half a dozen gentlemen and ladies join them after the meal had started, fresh from the road.

A vision walked into the room, her head held high, and despite the fact that she had traveled such a distance, no weariness lined her face as he'd noticed with other ladies. Annabel stood for a moment in her rose colored gown and swept her eyes across the room as if she was looking for someone. Who? Him?

Henry exhaled with a small measure of annoyance that he had not managed to catch her glance. He felt the touch of a hand on his arm and turned to meet the expectant gaze of Countess Mielszenski.

"There is a Polish saying. I don't know if you know it," she said and ran her tongue far too slowly over her lips. "There are three things difficult to keep hidden. Fire, a cold, and love."

Henry winced.

"It's a good saying don't you think?"

At least she had moved her hand off his arm although she now stroked the handle of her fork in a most suggestive manner.

"Very amusing," Henry replied politely and flicked his gaze to catch a glimpse of Annabel as she sat down.

****

Annabel knew she was late for dinner. She hoped the meal would be over quickly. She sat down with a young gallant on one side and an old roué on the other. It was at times like these she most wished she could be the simple country girl not the sophisticate they all thought she was and they always played up to.

At last dinner was over! Annabel pushed her chair back and drifted with her companions towards the double doors which had been opened into the next room. At exactly the right moment she drew back, let her companions move ahead, and pushed by the crowd too far forward before they realized they lost her. She sidestepped. Henry's arm was waiting.

She laid her hand on it and looked up at his face.

He smiled and she noticed the crinkles that appeared around his eyes. He was not that old. Around five and thirty she thought.

She liked his face and the detail on it. His chin was strong, as it should be, but not hard. His features were very even. The shape of his face was not oblong and yet not round.

"Mr. Champion," she said. It would be wiser to observe a formality of address. "I am obliged."

"Countess," he replied with a nod.

He led them forward out of the castle's dining hall and into the room which she knew ordinarily served as a grand drawing room. Now most of the furniture had been removed to make room for the party.

"I trust you have recovered from the journey," he said.

"What a foolish question! Did I look as if I was in need of a rest?"

"My apologies, Countess," he murmured, but she heard from his voice that it was tongue in cheek. "I forgot that you were an Amazon."

"I shall be kind and assume that you are giving me a compliment."

"Indeed. I never saw a lady ride so well."

For a moment Annabel thought she might blush. The sincerity that underscored his remark struck at her control.

"My father kept a fine stable," she said to distract herself out of it. "And so did my late husband."

"Sometimes things happen beyond our control." He paused and she heard him swallow. "Sometimes we cannot act as we ideally would like. Sometimes we must run in the direction fate pushes us."

Annabel did not know exactly what Henry was talking about but what he spoke could be the epitaph they would write about her life. "Everything you say is true but would it not be a fine thing if it were not true?" she said. "If it were always possible to act as we would like."

"Perhaps. But without compromise there is no order. And without order there is chaos and society cannot exist."

But there is already chaos, she wanted to say. *Wrongs go unpunished, murderers walk free and become powerful and are unchallenged.*

Instead she said as they were out of earshot from anyone, "I married the Count Szalynski because I feared I had no choice. I had already disgraced myself by being seen in Hyde Park alone riding with a rake following me. I thought I only had to engineer an appropriate situation with Freddy Hepplethwaite, as I believed he had feelings for me. I was too green to know that the Hepplethwaites' son and heir had been betrothed practically since birth to a neighboring landowner's daughter in Yorkshire."

"None of us are perfect," Henry replied with simplicity and she knew that she could trust him. It was instinctive, like the way she had taken his arm just now, knowing it would be a safe harbor.

"You know people may see us together and talk," she said. It was true; she had noticed a few glances in their direction.

"Is it so much of a scandal that you should be on my arm? I am, after all, your fellow countryman. What could be more natural?"

Annabel bit her lip. What could she say? Zakonski already knew Henry had visited her alone in Krakow. To fan any fire further would not be wise. The last thing she wanted to do was place Henry in danger. It had seemed the most natural thing in the world to take Henry's arm but in public there had been no sign that they were any more than the briefest of acquaintances. "You had better leave me for now. Perhaps later we might meet...in private?"

Annabel gently removed her hand from his arm against its will. It would have preferred to remain there.

"As you wish," he said and bowed formally in front of her. "Though before I leave you I must say what I meant to say earlier with my rather philosophical speech, that it is possible we may have to return to England very shortly."

"No. Not yet." She shook her head.

"But Szalynski has returned?"

"My chamber is on the second floor." She spoke
rapidly, little louder than a whisper. "On the
opposite side of the castle from here. If you go up the
stairs to the right of the tower and through a long
gallery there is a corridor to your left, and my room
is the third door on the right. Knock four times
quickly and I will know it is you."

"Countess." He smiled, bowed again and left her.

Chapter Eleven

Henry stopped and watched her walk away and join the conversation of a group of ladies close by. He cast his gaze over the company; some stood, some seated, some were still moving to where they wanted to be. He spied Marek in the midst of a group of gentlemen and ladies and he started towards them.

"Mr. Champion?"

Damn! He thought he had managed to shake off the Countess Mielszenski but here she was at his side looking at him with wide eyes like an irritating child.

"Countess," he said, keeping his voice polite but formal.

"I saw you here alone and thought perhaps I should keep you company," she said and tried to catch his eye.

He kept his gaze high, out of reach. "Please don't let me keep you from your friends."

"Oh! Are all Englishmen as uppity as you are, Mr. Champion? Was dinner not to your satisfaction?" She laughed, not an unpleasant laugh—it sounded like the tinkle of a small bell—but contrived nonetheless.

If she wants me to take her to bed, she is in for a long wait. He said, "Dinner was perfectly to my satisfaction, thank you."

"Oh, so stiff! So formal! Is this the way of all Englishmen?"

A loud voice carried across the entire room: their host, Count Szalynski. It saved Henry from having to answer.

"Ah, he's shouting for Pan Ryszelwski to fetch his balalaika and play a mazurek. The ladies are demanding it," the countess whispered boldly, slipping her arm into his.

A young lady, who stood next to Szalynski, clapped her hands together and said something clearly in approval.

A tall, thin man nodded to Szalynski and departed swiftly; the guitar playing Ryszelwski no doubt.

"It appears the musicians who were supposed to be here have not yet arrived," the Countess said. "Are you up to dancing a mazurek, Mr. Champion?"

"I have not yet had the pleasure of that dance," Henry replied. He'd be damned if he would allow her to hoodwink him into dancing with her. If there was to be dancing he could follow then he would like to dance with Annabel. Henry cast his gaze about the room and couldn't see her. Had she retired already? So very early?

"It is a fast dance, more complex dance than the stately polonaise. You know the polonaise of course?"

"Of course." He had danced the polonaise in Vienna and Paris. No doubt it would be in London by the time he got home.

Another cry from their host. Count Szalynski bowled towards a new arrival, embraced him and laughed. The room quieted somewhat as people took in this latest scene, Henry noted with interest. What was it about that man that set a room, like teeth, on edge? Count Zakonski had arrived.

Henry pulled at his glove to straighten it. The arrival of Count Zakonski seemed unlikely to make things simpler—rather the opposite.

****

Annabel blinked and caught her breath. So Zakonski had dared come here. Why? What was he up to?

Pan Ryszelwski had found his balalaika, settled it on his knee and began to play. Ewa Berekowski and her betrothed, Count Weczlewski, spun into the center of the room where the crowds had parted. Other couples sped to join them.

"Countess." Zakonski came beside her, bearing his teeth in a grin.

Annabel trembled. Her stomach had knotted. She thought she might be sick.

Zakonski had her arm in a moment, drew her towards him, and then towards the dancing. She wanted to break away but the shock of his arrival held her in thrall while she raced to recover her wits.

"I am too tired to dance the mazurek tonight," she said. "Please excuse me."

"A pity." Zakonski let go of her arm, drew back and bowed. "I look forward to dancing with you tomorrow."

He knew how to behave in company. He would not try anything here. She hoped.

****

Countess Mielszenski was swept into the dance by a young gallant. Henry was grateful and made his way with all speed over to Marek.

"Henry, can I present Count Gronowski?" Marek said with a flourish of his hand. He continued in French. "A fine fellow and also a hussar. Gronowksi, this is Mr. Henry Champion who fought at Waterloo with the great Duke of Wellington and was also part of the British delegation at Vienna."

"In some circles, Mr. Champion, you would be shot." Gronowski spoke French fluently and raised his winged eyebrows. "We rather liked Napoleon. Too short of stature to be king of Poland but he gave us our liberty and tried to give the Russians a good hiding."

"Many people in England admired Napoleon too," Henry replied. "But his continental system stopped us trading with Europe."

"English commerce is greedy," Gronowski goaded. "You have an empire to trade with, why did you need Europe too?"

"English gentlemen liked their French wines too much to let it pass, I think," Marek said. "And English ladies, perhaps their Paris fashions?"

Henry barked with laughter despite himself.

"Yes, I am imaging it in London now that you can get decent claret again without having to resort to smugglers and their very inferior stuff."

"The price for Poland." Gronowski's eyes narrowed.

"Come, Gronowski," Marek said, "We should admire the English and their liberty. It is Russia, Austria and Prussia who did not want there to be a Poland. We cannot blame the English for wanting to protect their own interests and agreeing to this peace in Europe."

Gronowski snorted but the corners of his mouth twitched into a grin. He thumped Henry on the back. "Right, you claret drinking Englishman, let's see how you fare on our Hungarian wines and Polish vodka. Poland may have gone from the map, but here at castle Szalynski we can prove to you it lives on."

****

Henry waited until later, some hours later. So late he thought at any moment he might see the beginning of the dawn and hear a cock crowing. The castle had quieted at last. He'd tried not to drink so much of the wine and the vodka but it had been difficult. He had become tipsy he knew, but Robards found a servant who had brought strong coffee to his chamber. Now he was awake and his head felt heavy as the aftereffects of his indulgence began to set in.

The castle was a maze of a place! Henry stole through the dimly-lit corridors, down and up stairs, retracing his steps several times until he was sure he was at the right room.

He raised his knuckles and tapped on the thick door four times in quick succession.

Nothing. He was sure this would be the right room. Was she somewhere else? In someone else's chamber? He screwed his face up as a pulse of pain ricocheted through his head. He had a headache setting in.

He heard the drawing back of a bolt and the door was opened no more than an inch. "Come in," she whispered.

Henry pushed the door open slightly wider, wincing at the loud creak, and slipped through into a bedchamber a similar size to his own. A large room with a large tester bed with its head against the wall on the left. On the right was a hearth with a dying fire, which provided the only light save for the single taper on a chest beside her bed. It was enough light to illuminate her loveliness so that he wanted to take her into his arms there and then and make her his. He felt the hard stab of pain in his chest: the knowledge he couldn't.

"You came," she whispered, "but it is so late."

A smile tugged at the corners of her mouth. She moved from where she was standing in front of the fire to the chaise by her window.

She was, he noted, still dressed in the rose-colored gown. Had he hoped, secretly, to find her *dishabille*? He still wore his full evening clothes. He had, of course, had to creep through the castle.

"Quite an adventure finding my way here," he told her and brushed a piece of lint that caught his eye from his sleeve.

"Now you made it, do you wish to sit down?" Her eyes seemed very dark and reflected the orange flicker of the flames. He was drawn into them, like a moth to a candle.

"Thank you," he said not paying any attention to himself speaking as he noticed how her bare arms, neck and countenance seemed luminous yet calm.

No blushing maiden then; blushing because she was alone at night with a gentleman in her bedchamber. Henry drew himself to attention, pushed his shoulders back and caught her now curious gaze. What had she just said? He hadn't been listening.

"I cannot, I am afraid, offer you anything by way of refreshment." She tilted her head fractionally to one side and wore a slight frown.

"I've had quite enough Polish hospitality for one evening," Henry replied and hiccoughed. Damn. He pressed his hand against his mouth.

"Oh." She frowned. She walked up to him and with a gentle hand on his shoulder guided him to the chaise.

Whoever furnished this room had not anticipated a need for separate chairs. There was only one chaise-longue. Henry was sure in his own chamber there were a pair of chairs. He wasn't sure he wanted to sit next to her on the very same chaise, but sat there anyway as she gently guided him over.

"Henry," she said catching his eye as he sat down, "are you drunk?"

"No." He could look at her straight and luckily the hiccough had not been followed by another. "I was decidedly tipsy earlier but it has gone past that now and I am getting the very devil of a headache."

He rubbed his temples and her hand caught his, laid it down and with her soft fingers she pressed gently on the sides of his forehead. Henry closed his eyes, concentrated on the sensation. If only she could sooth the rollicking pain away.

"You need to sleep," she whispered.

I want you to be my wife so you do this every time I am foolish with the bottle. Perhaps he was still a little tipsy.

"You'll feel better in the morning. The worst may well have passed."

"It is nearly morning." Henry laughed. She removed her hands and he opened his eyes.

Annabel leaned back towards the window and he watched the way the material of her dress pulled so he could admire the curve of her breast. She twitched the curtains and looked out.

"Yes, I can see the beginnings of streaks of light outside."

"Have you been waiting up for me all this time?"

Annabel let the curtain fall. "Yes," she said sitting back down so she faced him. "I wanted to speak with you about something important."

He shifted, stretched his hands out on his lap and then let them settle again.

"I am listening," he said.

"You will have seen, I think, that Zakonski is here. I do not know why he has come but I fear there will be trouble."

All the more reason to go back to England without delay. He said, "Have you spoken to Szalynski about it?"

"No, but I will do so tomorrow. He will be on his guard though, no matter how friendly he seems towards Zakonski in person. Szalynski knows his true colors."

A shout came from the corridor. A door banged. Another shout. Her gaze flicked from Henry to the door to her room, her immediate fear that it would fling open.

What was going on? She strained to hear. More creaking and banging and the heavy footsteps of someone running, now more than one person was running.

There was more shouting, from just outside in the corridor.

Annabel's breath caught. Why, now of all times?

"What is it?" Henry leaned forward.

"Wolves."

Henry started.

More shouting rattled through the castle.

"A pack of wolves have surrounded the village," Annabel explained from what she could pick up from the commotion. "The men are all getting their guns and going to shoot them."

"I should go too?"

"You should go. You might be missed." She wished she could have said otherwise. "Henry, be careful. The wolves must be desperate if they have massed on the village."

Henry stood up and pulled a pistol from beneath his coat. Annabel gasped. She was startled to see that he was armed even in evening dress.

"I'll see you later," he said and smiled ruefully. He stepped forward, bent down and brushed his lips on her forehead. She closed her eyes as her skin tingled.

She opened her eyes and looked up to see he wore a serious expression.

"Until later," he said.

She nodded, couldn't bring herself to speak before he left the room. She pressed her fingers through her hair and onto her head that throbbed with tiredness and emotion.

She threw herself down onto her bed, grasping fistfuls of the damask counterpane in her hands and wept.

****

The village below the castle was like so many Henry had seen. The largest building the church, and the rest a scattered cluster of small wattle houses covered in thick grayish-white or egg-shell blue plaster. The fences that kept in their milk cows and chickens were made from sapling twigs, woven like baskets, not made with planks like English fences.

"Now the wolves have taken every chicken from the outlying farms they have grown bolder and more desperate," Count Gronowski said under his breath. "And they will not shy of taking a child if the opportunity arises."

More than a dozen gentlemen had assembled in the great hall of the castle and the plan had been decided. Certainly not all the male guests at the castle were here, but then Henry had learned that a number of gentlemen had already left some time ago for a hunting expedition after boar. Even though it was still dark and they had stealthily hurried down the road to the village, Henry could not believe the wolves did not know they were coming. It was pleasantly refreshing to breathe the cold night air. His head still hurt but felt clearer.

He crouched now with Marek and Gronowksi behind a house where they brewed beer. A sweet smell tickled his nostrils and Henry fought the urge to sneeze.

Then they heard it. A howl pulsed through the air and was answered.

Right in front of them a four-legged creature, like a large dog, his eyes glinting in the moonlight and his tail tucked between his legs, padded through the street. Another two wolves followed him.

Henry heard a click. One of his companions had cocked their pistol. He did the same.

Piercing through the darkness came a woman's screams. His gaze was drawn to the noise and even though it sounded close by he could not make out the house it came from. Beyond their immediate vision, even the outlines of houses were lost to the dimness.

"God in heaven, there's a wolf pounding at her door and she has a baby," Marek growled in translation.

Crack!

As if waiting for their cue pistol shots exploded all around them.

There was barking and yelping, further shots. Henry saw one of the wolves skid around and start to flee. The animal was in his sights and he aimed, fired and it dropped to the ground, stone dead.

"Twelve, we got twelve of them," Gronowski said later on their way back to the castle. "But a number got away."

To Henry it didn't seen wholly fair to kill an animal who was only doing what was its nature. Yet what if it had been his house, his baby?

"I know one wolf that got away," Marek said in English under his breath.

Henry followed the direction of Marek's gaze and caught the flash of those familiar teeth. Count Zakonski, looking as pleased as punch, was stomping up the hill in a hearty conversation with Count Szalynski. Zakonski slapped Szalynski on the back and the gesture was returned. How friendly were they? Henry wondered.

Chapter Twelve

Thank heavens Polish coffee was so deliciously thick and strong. Henry picked up the delicate Dresden cup he had already laced with cream and took a determined gulp.

And thank heavens that this was the kind of breakfast that the hunting fraternity demanded. An informal repast of enormous proportions served in the ballroom close to midday.

And thank heavens for Robards who had got him out of bed and dressed in time.

The green-jacketed hunters who could not have slept a wink as they left the castle before the wolf hunt and only just returned this last hour were in fine spirits and mostly, it seemed, arguing.

Some people sat for breakfast, mostly ladies— some stood, mostly gentlemen. Henry saw Countess Mielszenski seated and in conversation. She did not notice him. That was fortunate. He looked about but could not see Annabel anywhere. He took his plate, piled high with slices of a juniper smoked ham he had a craving for, and coffee cup, and balanced them on a window sill at the far side of the room.

He was somewhat afraid of sitting down just yet until he was absolutely sure he was awake. Count Weczlewski, one of the hunters, strode up to him. A young handsome-faced man whose betrothal to the waifish daughter of a certain Count Berekowski's had been the subject of much gossip and speculation.

"You didn't join us on the hunt, Mr...?" Weczlewski addressed him in French.

"Champion," Henry replied. "No, but we had a

little impromptu hunt of our own. Wolves."

"So I heard, and more successful than ours for boar. Did you get one?"

"Yes I did."

"Good." Weczlewski raised his coffee cup in a mock toast. "Tell me, how is the sport in England?"

"No boar or wolves, hares and foxes mostly, and in some places, stags."

"The boar hunt," Count Gronowski said, appearing on Weczlewski's right-hand side, "so I hear was a disaster."

"Someone told the boar we were coming so they were hiding." Weczlewski laughed. "You know there is nothing so unpredictable as a boar!"

Gronowski laughed. It must be a private joke.

"Wild boar, unpredictable. In the Polish language it's the same word," Weczlewski explained. He went on to explain in detail how the boar hunt had unfolded. Henry listened politely.

"Henry?"

Henry turned to see Marek just behind him.

"Come with me," his friend said in a low growl.

"What? Now?" Henry took a long gulp of his coffee.

"Yes," Marek replied testily.

Henry looked at the plate of ham in dismay but obediently followed Marek out of the room and through a series of doors and corridors until they came into a tiny courtyard. The sort of place servants might do washing, not a yard where guests were supposed to wander.

"What is it?" Henry asked. Marek's countenance was twisted and unhappy looking. He had put his arm out to lean on the door post, his fingers curled around it. They were taut, white at the knuckles.

"You know everyone knows you went to Countess Szalynski's bedchamber last night, don't you?" Marek said. From his tone of voice it wasn't a question, it was an accusation. What had bitten Marek? Henry tried to force his mind to wake up properly, start it working as if it were a clock that needed winding.

"No," Henry said in an even manner. "I—"

"Did you think you were the only person creeping about last night up to no good? It does not matter what the truth is, if you are actually lovers or not, the point is that everyone now thinks you are."

"But—"

"Not that I don't wish you your bit of fun, Henry, but things are not as simple as you see them. I wish to be firmly on the road to Paris within the month."

"What on earth do you mean?" Henry asked.

"Zakonski will kill you, if that's what he's after and he thinks you are a serious rival." Marek's eyes narrowed. "Think, Henry, what a waste for your corpse to be buried for no good reason in a Polish field. He murdered her husband, you know."

"That was in a duel."

"It was, but I'm not the only person who suspects the duel was a farce. Point is, Zakonski is an animal. He's not a gentleman like you or I. If I gave you my word, I'd stand by it. And you would do the same. Not Zakonski. He has no notion of honor."

"Let us suppose," Henry said, pressing his fingers together, "that people would not believe that nothing of that nature happened. So what if Countess Szalynski and I are lovers...what of it?"

"So you were in her bedchamber last night?"

"Yes I was. Briefly."

"Damn." Marek's expression creased even further. He ran his fingers through his hair. "I had hoped it might be a fabricated rumor, not one grounded in reality."

"We are not lovers."

Marek slammed his hand against the wall. "Why aren't you listening? *That* does not matter."

Henry took a deep breath. "I am listening. So what should I do?"

"Flirt like hell with every lady here. And quickly; we all go home tomorrow! I know this may go against your nature and, in truth, I am surprised you've not bedded the countess yet. It's not your style, but stronger men have been tempted into far worse. But play the rake, think of Casanova as being your middle name. Get yourself a reputation for dalliance and Zakonski might overlook your indiscretion."

Henry sighed. What was he supposed to do? In England it would be easier. He could have called Zakonski out, found someone honorable to provide the pistols and make sure there was no funny business. He could have made Annabel his own. But Zakonski wasn't even a man of honor. And Annabel? He had no reason to think that she had any feelings for him in the same vein as he did for her. He didn't even think it would be on for a man such as he to expect anything. He was still the very ordinary Henry Champion. Even with the good deal of blunt he was being paid for his errand he would barely be able to buy back his inheritance, let alone begin to keep her in the style to which she had become accustomed. His chest suddenly felt as though it had a lead weight inside it.

"My friend, cease looking so tired and wan. There is the Countess Mielszenski for starters."

"I suppose..." Henry ventured.

"Ah ha! The very woman who may yet save your hide. Quick, Henry, flirt with her, and under Zakonski's nose. She'll lap it up and I am sure if you want to go all the way, she'd be accommodating. Could you slip into her bedchamber tonight, do you think?"

"No."

"Come on! What about you just pretend to have

been there. Hang about her door until someone spots you and then just hurry away looking as guilty as sin?"

"I'll think about it."

"That's the spirit!" Marek smiled, though to Henry's mind it appeared somewhat forced. "Come, let's see what entertainment Szalynski has planned for today."

****

The dawn had broken by the time she must have fallen asleep but Annabel did not wake until after midday. She felt wretched even she knew it was only a dream. She had dreamt that they had been in the forest and Henry was attacked by a wolf. He'd lost so much blood that he was unconscious and everybody said they did not know if he would live. All she could see in her mind was a picture of Henry's body lying motionless on the ground, his blood seeping into the hard earth of the forest floor.

She came downstairs to find only a scattering of people still breakfasting. Kasimir Czorewicz, a young blade, fetched her a coffee and told her about the wolf and boar hunts as she drank. No one, he assured her, had been hurt or injured in any way. He offered her his arm as soon as she had finished and they walked to the great hall where everybody seemed to be assembling.

Henry had certainly not been mauled by a wolf. He stood looking as handsome and unscathed as ever beneath a tapestry depicting the hunting of a large bear. He was in a merry conversation with Countess Mielszenski and Countess Gronowski. Her chest constricted. She drew in a ragged breath. She would have liked to have been where Countess Mielszenski stood, so close they were almost touching. Of course she couldn't.

She buried her nose in her coffee for a moment, took a long sip and let her eyes shut briefly. What did she want? To play the game, as Countess Mielszenski did, in the hope that Henry would make her his mistress? She had vowed she would not marry again.

It was a strange twist of fate. So many men had wanted to bed her, and she had always refused without a qualm. She'd never been tempted. The one man who had come along and tempted her made what should be so simple utterly confusing. All the more so, because he was so important to her.

She looked up and caught the flash of Zakonski's teeth. He stood at the other side of the room, perfectly positioned to watch who entered and everything that was going on. He saw her. Annabel shivered and cast her eyes to the floor.

"Are you cold?" Czorewicz enquired. "Shall I find a servant to fetch you something else to wear?"

"Oh? No—" Annabel stopped as a gentleman stepped in front of her.

"Good morning, Annabel." Marek bowed. "Czorewicz,"

"Ralenski." Czorewicz let his arm drop, deferring to his senior.

"Why, thank you," Marek said with a grin.

"Good morning, Count Ralenski." Annabel took his arm. If Czorewicz deferred to Marek he would be even less a match for Zakonski. There was a good chance that Marek would delight in not passing her over to Zakonski should the situation arise. "I hear that the wolves were vanquished."

"Yes, it is to be hoped we killed enough of them so they think twice about worrying the village again," Marek said. "On the other hand the poor fellows who set out in the middle of the night after boar had very poor sport indeed. Szalynski's probably shot all the boar in his forest already."

"What do we do today?" Annabel asked.

"I have no idea." Marek shrugged his shoulders.

"What does one usually do at these parties? Hunt of course. Perhaps play some games."

Count Szalynski moved past them and into the middle of the room. He clapped his hands together and the conversations going on around the room halted.

"A game! A game for the men, but mostly for the amusement of the ladies." Count Szalynski swept his arms in the air. "We go to the forest for flowers."

"Flowers?" This shout came from Count Gronowski who stood beside Henry.

"I would make it a mushroom gathering competition but you know it's April, the wrong time of year." Szalynski shrugged his large shoulders. "This game is the idea of one of the ladies."

"Huzzah," Count Weczlewski called.

"Whichever gentleman brings back the finest posy of flowers shall be seated this evening next to the lady of his choice," Szalynski said. "And whichever lady of all the ladies makes the best garland of flowers will be seated next to the gentleman of her choice."

"Szalynski has been in Russia too long," someone close to her muttered. "He is losing his mind."

"And if we are blessed with a lucky coincidence," Szalynski continued, "and the makers of the best posy and the best garland wish to sit next to each other, then perchance cupid will also join us at dinner this evening!"

"What are you trying to do, Szalynski?" called out Count Gronowski. "Make maids of the flower of Polish manhood?"

Szalynski threw his head back and bellowed with laughter. "Come, Gronowski, you've had your sport." He clapped his hands as two menservants came into the room each carrying a large pile of willow baskets.

"To the forest!" Weczlewski motioned with his left arm and with his right took the hand of his betrothed, Ewa, who stood beside him.

"And bring your pistols, gentlemen," Gronowski shouted. "This flower picking won't take all afternoon. Come on, wife. I need your help. I don't know a daffodil from a bluebell."

There was much laughter and it seemed to be a cue for a general pairing off of ladies and gentlemen. Annabel felt her chest tighten as she watched Henry offer his arm to Countess Mielszenski. If only—

"Will you accompany me to the forest to look for flowers?" Marek bowed gallantly before her.

"I should be delighted," Annabel replied.

Marek darted off and fetched a basket. A smile pulled at her lips as she saw Zakonski stop in his tracks as Marek gave her his arm again.

It was firm underfoot in the forest; they kept to the well-worn paths. Annabel carried the basket and directed Marek which flowers to pick.

"Which flowers do you want in your posy?"

"Which flowers do you like?" he asked.

"There are some bluebells over there. They could make a pretty posy."

Marek bounded off dutifully.

"No, no, no! Pick them at the very base of their stems." Annabel bent down beside the clump of bluebells to show him. "Like this."

She felt Marek's breath at the back of her neck as she rose. She stepped to the side. He was too close, and his gaze was too intense.

"Marek?" she said.

"Annabel."

She had dropped the basket on the ground and felt a crimson heat run up her neck. She knew what he was thinking; there was no need for words. Dozens of men had looked at her in such a way. It meant they wanted her in their bed. She should be used to it now.

He swooped down to pick up the basket. She found she was breathing very quickly. She liked Marek, she trusted him, but she did not want to be his lover.

"Marek, do not think of me in that way. We are friends, that is all."

"Only friends?" He paused and then handed the basket back to her. "Is it not that you like Henry the better?"

"You know that is not what this is about. Zakonski—"

"Do not worry about him. I will kill him if he lays a finger on you."

"Marek!"

"As for Henry, pay him no heed. He is a rake. Watch how he flirts with Countess Mielszenski, whom he only met yesterday. Do not forget I knew him in Paris and in Vienna. There was a lady—well, lady is too grand word for her—a woman in Vienna called Giselle with whom he conducted the most shameful affair."

"Oh, Marek—"

"I do not proposition you in an ignoble way, my sweet one." He flung himself on his knees, seized her hands and held them in his. Annabel trembled. Was what he said about Henry true? Was he like all the rest of them, merely looking to take what he wanted before casting her aside and moving on to the next conquest?

"Annabel, I am a gentleman of honor. I offer you marriage. To a Polish gentleman of good family and excellent fortune. I go to London, very soon, and would have you join me if you are willing. Now Aleksander is back from Russia he can deal with Zakonski. The time will come when we will free Poland again. I am sad to say it but that time is not yet now."

It was everything she should want. Yet she had sworn she would never marry again, and certainly not for convenience. She had married in haste before. She would learn from her mistakes, not make them again. She felt a tear prick the back of her eye.

And for all Marek's vainglorious proclamations, she knew Zakonski would kill him if he could. She would not wish that fate on any man, especially one who had been so kind to her.

"I cannot marry you, Marek," she said. "And I know you will respect my decision, not press me any further on the matter and yet remain a true friend."

"Of course," Marek replied, letting go of her hand and standing up very straight. He clicked his heels. "Zakonski needs to be taught a lesson. Has he threatened you? I have my pistol with me. I will kill him now."

"Marek, wait. No, he has done nothing. Nothing, yet." She touched his arm and found she was trembling. "Thank you, Marek. You are a kind, kind friend." She meant it. The way his face closed told her that he wanted, perhaps more than marriage, to tempt her into his bed. But he had wisely decided to leave the subject for now. She did not think he was the kind of man to force the issue but she had better be careful. She would take Helena with her to London and perhaps one of her footmen too. More than ever she wanted to go home to England. Though she could never return to her childhood and those happy years in the nursery before she really understood what it meant not to have a father and mother. She'd lived in different houses, at the whim of indifferent relatives, never really wanted or cherished anywhere. Only her aunt had been truly kind to her and wanted her again now. In England, she would have some kind of family. She could have a life free of worry, free of Zakonski.

"I shall rein in my temper for the moment and

venture to say you might be right. Perhaps there is a
better way, a way that can be found to discredit
Zakonski." Marek's expression was so fierce it was
terrible. Annabel believed he meant every word he
said. "His humiliation would be harder for him to
bear, I think perhaps, than death."

****

Countess Mielszenski ran her tongue lightly
over her lips and then pouted as she spoke. "What a
delightful little flower!" She motioned her arm to the
left, cocked her head and puffed her chest out. "I
wonder what it is called. What is it in English?"

"I have no idea," Henry replied giving the plant
which grew sheltered half under an old fallen tree no
more than a cursory glance. She was grating on him
now. He had thought she would but he'd better put
up with it.

"Too pale for a posy." She wrinkled her nose
slightly. He was no doubt supposed to find such a
gesture attractive.

"What about your garland?" he said.

"Oh, I don't know the first thing about such
things. At our place the servants arrange the
flowers. Ha, look over there—many bluebells."

Getting to the bluebells meant leaving the path.
Although stepping through the new ferns and mossy
undergrowth was nothing to Henry, Countess
Mielszenski shrieked when she stepped on a large
twig and it snapped.

"Oh, dear, I am not sure I can go on. I'm
frightened."

Henry didn't hear her. He had caught the sound
of voices to their left and was looking at the
damndest of sights being played out before him.
Annabel standing in the forest, and on his knees
before her and holding her hands in his own, Marek.

Every hair on the back of Henry's neck stood on
end.

"Annabel, I offer you marriage...." Henry didn't catch the rest of Marek's speech but it was enough. His fists clenched and red spots danced in front of his eyes but his feet were rooted to the ground. He couldn't move.

What she said in return he couldn't hear, her voice was too low. Nor Marek's reply. They appeared to be having some kind of discussion. Then her words rang out clearly.

"No...yes. Yes..."

Had she agreed to marry Marek? And he'd thought Marek was his friend, warning him away from Annabel on the pretext that she was in danger from Zakonski. What a fool he had been.

"Mr. Champion? Help! I'm frightened!"

Henry reluctantly tore his gaze away and turned around to see Countess Mielszenski standing wide-eyed as if she was about to burst into tears.

Damn women! Give him a crowd of fellows even if they did bore him to death with their hunting tales; it was a damn sight better than messing with this duplicitous sex!

"Would it help if I carried you back to the path?" Henry said through gritted teeth.

Countess Mielszenski's lips broke into a smile. She fluttered her eyelashes and opened her mouth to speak—

A cacophony of shouting pierced through the trees.

The color drained from the countess's face. "A boar!" she screamed in French. "There's a boar!"

Chapter Thirteen

"A boar! There's a boar!" came the shouting.

"Quick!" Marek grabbed Annabel's hand. "Which is a good tree?"

She spun around, sizing up the various trees. Which one would hold them and withstand being attacked by a boar if the animal turned nasty?

She stopped in her tracks at the sight of Henry running towards them with Countess Mielszenski in his arms.

"Come on," Marek said. "What about that one?"

"Henry," Annabel muttered.

"Let Henry find his own damn tree." Marek heaved his shoulder against the large oak tree but it wasn't going anywhere.

"Marek!" Annabel shouted at him. He made her very cross. Henry was supposed to be his friend and he was his guest in a foreign country.

"Oh, maybe he doesn't know what to do when there's a boar," Marek conceded. He waved at Henry who had almost reached them. "Henry, with a boar you must find a tree. There is nothing else for it."

"Someone shoot the boar," came a shout from close by. Annabel couldn't see—the trees were thick in this part of the wood—but it sounded like Count Gronowski. "My second best brace of pistols to whoever shoots the boar."

Countess Mielszenski screamed as Henry put her down on her feet.

"I might faint!" she cried.

"No, you damn well won't," Henry said, scooping the countess up and throwing her up into the tree.

"Hold on to that branch and pull yourself up the tree, quickly," Marek barked at her in Polish.

"Henry, quick!" Annabel said. "Get up the tree!"

His eyes narrowed and he looked at her so coldly she quite forgot the boar for that moment and gulped in surprise.

"No, ladies first," he said motioning towards the tree.

The boar! Annabel swung herself up into the tree, felt Henry's arms on her back. They didn't need to be there—she knew how to climb a tree. Testing each branch for strength, she clambered up and settled herself on a very stout high branch opposite Countess Mielszenski. The silly woman could also climb a tree with rapidity when she put her mind to it.

Marek was with them a moment later, leaving only Henry on the ground. Testily, he swung himself up onto a low branch.

"Come on, Henry," Marek called.

"I can't even see a boar," Countess Mielszenski said. "It is probably Count Gronowski playing a trick."

"What is that over there then?" Marek pointed only a small distance away.

Annabel looked and saw the dark gray mound rushing forward through the undergrowth towards them. It was a big one—the size of a sheep. And Henry still wasn't high enough up the tree yet.

"Henry!" she screamed.

"Put your leg on that branch, the one to the right," Marek shouted to him as he loaded his pistol.

"I'm coming," Henry said, heaving himself up.

His back foot slipped. He lost his balance.

"The boar!" Countess Mielszenski shouted.

"Henry!" Annabel cried. Her dream was coming true except she'd lose him to a boar, not a wolf.

Henry was hanging on to the branch above him

for dear life. He somehow managed to swing his body so that he regained his footing again.

Crack!

The noise from Marek's pistol rang through the forest.

"Damn. Missed."

"Henry, pull yourself up! Quickly," Annabel shouted. She wished she could somehow reach down and help him.

Henry jumped—yes, jumped—up to the next branch, then pulled himself up another. Mary, mother of God, she prayed he was out of the boar's reach now.

Crack!

The second shot from Marek's pistol.

With a squeal that would have shattered glass, the boar fell to the ground just beneath them. The animal writhed a moment and died.

Annabel couldn't see now with the tears that streamed down in front of her eyes.

"That was a damn near run thing," Henry said.

"I won't say anything about your tree climbing accomplishments," Marek rejoined. "What on earth did you get up to when you were a boy?"

"Sailing mostly, and fishing. Most of it was in the West Indies. No trees like this there. Or wild boar for that matter!"

"Well, let's get down now we can," Marek said.

"Did someone shoot the boar?" came a shout in Polish from nearby.

"Yes, the boar is dead!" Marek shouted back.

Annabel sniffed. She hadn't bought a handkerchief with her so there was nothing for it but to wipe away her tears with the sleeve of her jacket. She needed to be able to see to get back down the tree.

Back down on the ground, Henry offered her a clean handkerchief.

"Thank you," she said and blew her nose. "I was worried."

"About me?" The way he said it with a strange laugh did not sound right but she couldn't read anything from his eyes. They were closed, somehow, as if they were complete strangers.

Annabel went to pick up her basket from where she had left it on the forest floor. She kept her back to the boar as several people arrived and discussed what had happened. She didn't like seeing it lying there.

"I take it we are taking the boar back to the castle," Count Gronowski said.

"How much does it weigh? Can we carry it between us?" Marek said.

Gronowski snorted his answer.

"Henry, you go with Czorewicz and take the ladies back to the castle," Marek said in English. "The rest of us will manage the boar." He turned to the others. "I still think we will end up having to drag it to the path and get a man to come with a cart for it," he said in Polish.

"Bells and whistles! And you call yourself a hussar!"

"What about the flowers?" Countess Gronowski ventured.

"Flowers?" her husband answered. "I say Ralenski wins the prize. A boar like this beats a posy of flowers one hundred times over."

"Come on, we can collect things for our garlands on the way back," one of the young ladies said. A gaggle of girls bounded ahead back towards the path.

"I feel a little faint," Countess Mielszenski said.

"Here, take my arm," Czorewicz replied.

Annabel stiffened. She would not have minded Czorewicz's arm to lean on herself. She could make a similar remark and no doubt Henry would feel

obliged to offer her his arm but she would not stoop
so low. She was not a flirt. She was quite recovered
now, she told herself, and took some steps forward,
taking care not to put her footing on any of the
slippery moss-covered stones.

"Are you quite all right?" Countess Gronowski
asked, coming up behind her.

"I was a bit shaken but that has passed now,"
Annabel replied. "I thought the boar might reach
Mr. Champion. He was not yet far enough up the
tree as the boar charged towards us."

"That must have been quite frightening."

"It was." Annabel shuddered at the memory.

"I do hope you are not taking my name in vain,"
Henry said, appearing at her right and looking at
her with very cold eyes.

"Of course not!" Annabel snapped back. She
didn't even feel like speaking English to him, she
stuck to French. "I was just telling Countess
Gronowski how frightened I was when I thought the
boar might get you."

She immediately regretted her waspishness. He
was in a strange temper it was true but she was, she
admitted to herself, still shaken.

"Your concern for my safety is touching," he said
in a cavalier fashion. "At least Marek was far up the
tree. That would have been...your main concern."

"What on earth is the matter with you?"
Annabel found she couldn't keep her temper from
her voice. Not now that Henry seemed determined to
goad her with some kind of nonsense she didn't even
understand.

"What's the matter with me? You really want to
know? Well, I come within a hair's breadth of being
savaged by a boar and I discover the woman I love is
marrying someone else. All in all it's not been a good
day."

The woman I love? Annabel stumbled, stepped

on a piece of rotten bark. It collapsed. She swayed—into Henry's arms.

"Here, I've got you," he said. She felt his lips brushing at her hair just above her ear. "Well, I've got you for the moment."

She wanted to whimper, nestle up to him, and stay there—preferably forever.

She made do with staying absolutely still, relying on the feel of his strong arms, and bathing in the heat from his body. She felt the rise and fall of his chest and heard his unsteady breathing and the rapid beats of his heart.

A sudden panic started to grow in her breast. What if Zakonski was somewhere watching, or this was reported back to him?

"I can...stand," she said pulling herself away.

She saw Henry stiffen as he stepped back. He'd had spots of color on his cheeks before, but now he looked drained.

Who was this woman who Henry loved? Countess Mielszenski? He had only met her yesterday. Countess Mielszenski was not betrothed to anyone to her knowledge. She tried to think who was getting married. Ewa Berekowski? No, how could it be her?

"Can I offer you my arm?" he said.

"Thank you... Just to the path." Annabel rested her fingers on his sleeve, hardly daring to touch him.

Was it a lady from England? Or somewhere else? Perhaps he had received news. But, no, that did not seem likely that a letter would find its way to Henry here today, unless a servant had brought it all the way from Krakow.

It must be Countess Mielszenski. He had sat next to her at dinner last night and she had seen him talking to her before they set out to the forest. And he had enough time with her alone in the forest to get up to all sorts of mischief. Perhaps Henry had offered her his hand and she had turned him down by saying she was marrying someone else. Annabel thought that Countess Mielszenski was quite capable of bending the truth if it suited her.

"I'm sorry," Annabel said. Her heart felt like lead but it would be mean of her not to offer him some comfort. Henry was a friend wasn't he?

"For what?" He sounded surprised.

"To hear about the woman."

She thought she heard the crunch of his teeth as he stopped himself saying whatever he was about to say next.

"Ah, here we are. The path." She tried to keep her voice sounding bright even though she wanted to lay her head down on the ground and weep. "I can manage by myself now very well. Thank you, Henry."

****

"Come on, that's the third cravat gone to waste! How difficult is it to tie an Oriental?"

Henry looked at himself in the mirror and watched the back of Robards head bobbing about in front of him. Poor Robards, he was thinning a bit on top. At least that was something he didn't have to worry about. His own thick locks were the spit of his father's and his pater had certainly had all his hair.

"Pretty difficult, 'specially as you keep moving, sir." Robards gave the neckcloth a firm tug.

"For heaven's sake! What are you trying to do? Strangle me!"

"What's bitten you, sir, if you don't mind my asking?" Robards spoke as if he had a mouthful of pins. "Fallen out with that countess?"

"What did you say?"

"A little bird told me that after you left her in order to hunt wolves last night she threw herself down on her bed and wept like Mary Magdalene."

"What little bird? Oh, that girl you've been after

145

I suppose, who's Countess Szalynski's maid? I should have guessed. Haven't you got anything better to do than sit about gossiping like an old woman?" Henry found himself smiling regardless. "Such as practicing tying Orientals?"

"Don't need the practice, sir. There we are. Done." Robards stepped back.

"Excellent," Henry said admiring Robards' efforts in the mirror. He would cut a fine dash tonight in his elegant English evening dress and have all the ladies swooning over him. He might be a plain mister but he was an English gentleman of a good family, well educated and feted at home as a minor hero of Waterloo.

He would be going home soon. Europe was charming but beneath the veneer it was all the same. It was time he faced up to a few things and got on with what he was supposed to be doing here.

He pushed his shoulders back so that he stood at his very tallest. First there was dinner and the betrayal of his best friend to get through.

****

"It has been decided among the gentlemen that the winner of the posy competition is Count Ralenski," announced Count Szalynski to the company assembled before dinner in the grand drawing room. "His, er, contribution was unorthodox and not pretty but certainly the biggest."

Annabel smiled, but could not quite bring herself to join in the raucous laughter.

"And the winner of the ladies garland competition is my own dear, sweet sister-in-law, Countess Szalynski."

Annabel's hand flew to her mouth. She had put a lot of effort into her garland she knew, but only because it had taken her mind off all the things she did not wish to think about.

"So, Ralenski and Countess Szalynski, the

company is waiting with bated breath to hear where you would sit?"

Marek took a step forward. "If it is permitted, sir, I would be honored to sit next to your sister..."

There were gasps from around the room.

"... Countess Szalynski?" Marek finished.

"Come, that is a low request, Ralenski," Grownoski shouted out. "The countess is also a winner and she too deserves to choose."

The crowd murmured approval.

"Why." Szalynski stretched his arms out. "Of course! I would happily have you pay attentions to my dear sister, Ralenski, but the decision rests with her. Countess?"

"Thank you," Annabel said in French. And now for her moment of utter stupidity. "But I choose Mr. Champion, the Englishman."

Annabel saw the surprise on Marek's countenance and caught the flash of Zakonski's feral gaze and shivered. She did not dare look at Henry. He seemed to have been avoiding her all day yet she felt compelled to be in his company if she could. She would dance with Zakonski later if she could bring herself to it. That should keep him satisfied enough. Strangely she felt less scared. Marek's plan, Marek's plan, Marek's plan, she kept repeating in her head.

"The pleasure would be mine," Henry said. When she finally looked towards him his expression was formal and he gave nothing away.

Several of the ladies clapped and exclaimed that she was wise. The Englishman was dashing, they said. Henry did look incredibly elegant that evening. Immaculate. And the cut of his clothes quite took the breath away.

"Ralenski, choose again. Now, let the celebrations begin," Szalynski bellowed and two footmen rushed forward to pull open the double doors to the dining hall.

Henry walked towards her and bowed in the formal manner before offering her his arm.

So many times she had taken his arm and yet it never got any easier. She felt a quiver at the base of her throat. Toes that should be happy in their silken slippers clenched.

She rested her hand in the middle of his arm. Always the same place, she mused, the very middle, over the top of the curve of his muscle. She allowed him to walk her forward, matching his pace exactly without having to think about it.

Annabel did not know what she could do so that it would always be so.

She should be overcome with happiness. Marek had a plan, a good plan. She could trust him as she remembered how Marek had been a trusted friend of her husband's. And yet she felt as if she had been plunged in a vat of freezing water.

It was nothing to do with Marek or Zakonski and everything to do with Henry. The knowledge of his interest in other women had shaken her so much because she loved him herself. She recognized it now. It had taken that, and witnessing his near run-in with the boar, that had made her realize the thing she was terrified of most of all was losing him.

Yet she didn't have him and didn't know what she could do. He had been attracted to her from the start all those years ago, and again here in Poland she was sure, but now he was so cold. He had even spoken the words that he loved another woman. Loved another woman *who was now lost to him.* Was there any way she could turn his attentions back onto herself? People could love more than once in their life could they not?

She should have pride. Shrug and say, *well, he loved another so he will never do for me.* But she would rather take a chance. At least then, she could say she tried.

They sat down.

She watched him take a swig of the vodka that was provided for all the gentlemen to drink. She picked up her spoon and dipped it into the barszcz. The crimson liquid was steaming and she let the soup burn her throat as she supposed his must be feeling from the vodka unless he was used to such strong spirits.

He turned, deliberately she thought, away from her to speak with the lady who sat next to him. Her chest constricted with pain. This was going to be hard, very hard.

Seated on her other side was Count Gronowski. A man one could at least have a conversation with she decided grasping for a morsel of refreshment in what seemed like a barren desert. This was a grand banquet and they would be at the table a very long time.

She sighed and played with her cutlery, then let her arm stray into his part of the table. Nothing. He still did not say anything or even look at her. She dropped her napkin but a footman darted to fetch her a fresh one before Henry even noticed.

She would have to be more direct, speak to him and then he could not ignore her.

"The centerpiece, Henry, it is very fine isn't it?" she said. It was a huge confection made of sugar cream, a winter landscape with cottages of cake and decorated with small china figures in Polish dress.

"Yes," Henry said and looked at her. His expression was unfathomable but she caught the flicker of his eyelashes, held his gaze.

"You still haven't told me very much about England," Annabel said and gave Henry what she considered was her sweetest smile. "What else has happened since I have been away?"

"England?" He turned towards her and placed his fork down. His expression remained serious. She had a sudden urge to beat her fists against him just to see if she could provoke a reaction. He could feel. She knew he felt things. "Well—"

"Some people are of the opinion that England is the greatest nation in the world," Count Gronowski growled over her shoulder. "The English!"

The chatter around the table from those closest to them seemed to fade away. Annabel stared at the cake.

Chapter Fourteen

One by one the conversation stopped until the whole room had fallen into a deep hush.

Annabel looked at Henry but his expression did not change. Not even when he spoke.

"My question is this then," he said, his voice even and calm. "If England is so fine a place then why I am here? Why do I want to explore other places and not sit at home and rake in my country's bounty?"

"A good question," Gronowski agreed. He smiled and nodded. Although from his tone Annabel thought he seemed to begrudge it slightly.

"Because the wealth comes not from within, but without. The empire. We are pirates. Plunder and exploitation."

"It's the same in Russia!" Gronowski picked up a goose leg. "Look at that country with its thousands of serfs. And the nobles, the rich ones, are even richer than even the richest of the English."

"Spot on," Henry said. "Even though slavery is banned in England itself we still allow it to go on in parts of the Empire."

"But wait." Annabel broke in. Her husband had been of the opinion that England was a great country, a country Poland should emulate. "The English parliamentary systems, the love of liberty, are the envy of the world."

"And your navy," Gronowski added. "We envy that."

"Yet we still send our children to break their necks on mill machinery and suffocate to death in coal mines."

"Is that really true?" Annabel asked. She was not sure she could believe it. Not England where every man was free.

"Of course it is true! I have already decided when I go back to England I am going to go into Parliament and do everything I can to have laws passed against such cruelties. Why can't English children frolic in the countryside like children here?"

Annabel was silent. Henry sounded so purposeful, so serious.

"Good on you," Count Gronowski said and raised his glass. "A toast. To your every success."

"Thank you," Henry replied. She saw him turn his attention back to the dill baked salmon and roasted carp on his plate. She felt so much for him that she ached.

"I hope you've tried the caviar. It's very good," Gronowski said. "All the way from the Caspian sea. Szalynski lays a good table, in the old Polish style."

"Yes, I have," Henry replied looking up again and over towards Gronowski. "Magnificent."

He watched Annabel take a sip of her wine and wanted those slender fingers that held the stem of her glass to be touching him. He noted every sinew of her throat as she swallowed and wanted to nuzzle and kiss every inch of it.

He pressed his foot hidden beneath the table into the floor and told himself to get a handle on his control.

What was she up to? Playing every trick she could think of it seemed to get his attention. Was that what she wanted? Didn't she know that he wanted her with a force so violent that if she continued to goad him he was liable to sling her over his shoulder right now and carry her upstairs? He desired to make love to her and to the devil with friendship and any other consequences.

So he would play her game. He couldn't help himself. He felt himself drawn to her, like a moth to a flame.

"Annabel," he whispered, drawing himself as close to her as he thought he could and still remain decent. She leaned towards him and he kept his voice very low so that only she could hear what he said. "Don't think I don't notice you, your every move. I was caught by your beauty like a butterfly in a net from the first and still you fascinate me."

She took a sharp intake of breath. He wondered if he dared take a tendril of her hair and play with it, winding it around his finger. Perhaps he shouldn't at dinner. He could reach her from where she was to him. He tried to congratulate himself on his admirable self-restraint while her scent, jasmine he thought, tickled his nose.

"Henry." She breathed his name and he knew he was lost.

Her hand seemed to be slipping from the table where it rested. He caught it as it fell to her lap and caressed the tops of her fingers with his own. Any lady of virtue should be scandalized. She did not move. He did not want her to.

The heat, the frission of something tangible burned through her gloves and his own. That they were in a crowded room now did not matter. Henry only saw, breathed, felt her, and wondered if he dared move his fingers upwards towards her wrist.

A dark shadow appeared over them.

"You English dog!"

Henry started back and his chair scraped the wooden floor. In a moment he was on his feet, facing his aggressor.

"Count Zakonski," he replied in French, "what an unexpected...pleasure."

Zakonski wore a face as dark as thunder.

"What do you think you are playing at?"

Zakonski bellowed each word, almost spat them out.

Henry stiffened. He had promised himself he would not draw attention to himself any more than was necessary, and certainly not get involved in any altercations. To his dismay, the noise in the room steadily fell towards another hush. He had the sinking feeling that this was going to be very public and very unavoidable.

"I am minded, dear count, to excuse your rather...abrupt interruption of my enjoyment of dinner." Henry raised an eyebrow pointedly. "It would appear that there may have been some misunderstanding?"

"Dog!" Zakonski shouted.

It sounded to Annabel like a growl from the beast that he was.

She looked around and saw that Marek had stood up and was coming towards them.

"I am sure there has been a misunderstanding!" Gronowski shouted. "Sit down, Zakonski, your sour face is spoiling my dinner."

"No misunderstanding." Zakonski gave a wide smile that seemed completely at odds with his knotted forehead. "Were it on my account I would be generous to our English guest, but this concerns a lady's honor."

She could not allow this to happen! How dare he! "Cou—"

Henry gave her a quelling stare.

"For the advantage you have taken of a lady's honor," Zakonski rasped. "I will see her honor satisfied in the traditional manner."

What was Henry going to do? Surely he must see how grave this was?

"What are you talking about, Zakonski?" Marek said, pushing his way past Annabel. He tried his best to look down his nose at the count although the two were of similar stature. "My friend, as you so eloquently pointed out, is English. He doesn't understand your riddles."

Zakonski inclined his head at Marek. "I will make myself plain." He stared back at Henry. "Mr. Champion." His voice was like iron. "I demand satisfaction."

Annabel wanted to scream. Henry stood completely still as if he had not even heard what Zakonski had said. He needed to do something. Someone needed to do something to make this impending nightmare go away.

If only Henry would say that they were engaged, or had an understanding or something, Zakonski would be humiliated and forced to withdraw his challenge. But they were not. Henry had never given her cause to think that his feelings for her were permanent. He stood so stiff, so unyielding, she wondered whether he ever would.

"Yes." Henry broke the silence with one simple word. Foolish, foolish man, Annabel wanted to scream at him and drag him away somewhere. "I accept."

"It would be my honor to provide the pistols," Marek said stepping forward into the space between Henry and Zakonski. Annabel's breath caught. "Though I have a beautiful pair of short swords at home, from the time of Jan Sobieski—"

"Not swords, pistols." Henry spoke with a sharp sounding calm. He gave a weak smile.

"Pistols then." Zakonski shrugged.

Annabel felt a sudden stab of confusion. Was the duel genuine? No, she knew Zakonski too well. The duel could not go ahead. Henry would be dead by Zakonski's hand by some means of foul play.

"Then, as I said, I will provide the pistols," Marek replied.

"We will meet in Krakow then," Zakonski said. "Not tomorrow but the day after."

"No." Marek put his hand out. "It would not be right to duel on a Sunday."

"On Monday then," Zakonski conceded, the line of his mouth thinning. "In Balice forest, just outside the city. My second will call on you Count Ralenski to inspect the pistols and arrange the details."

Marek nodded. Zakonski inclined his head likewise and then turned and walked away.

Still the crackle hung in the air. Henry stood, taut as an upstrung puppet, only his eyes moving.

Szalynski stood up where he sat some way away and clapped his hands. "The sport for now is over. If everyone has eaten enough for now, let us go to the dancing!"

At once the room exploded. Everybody of course would be exchanging their views on what had just occurred.

"What are you doing?" Annabel said to Henry, wishing she could pummel some life into him with her fists. "Zakonski will kill you—"

"Only if I fail to kill him first."

"Hush, Annabel. I have a plan," Marek said. "Do not worry. Henry will be fine."

"You know if I was a hot-blooded Italian or a crazy Russian I would demand satisfaction of you," Henry said to Marek, his eyes flashing suddenly. "Luckily for you I am sensible and English. And I need you as my second."

"What are you talking about, Henry?"

"Don't pretend you don't know!"

"No I don't know." Marek folded his arms in front of his chest.

"It is you Zakonski should be dueling with, not me. But don't worry I will do my best to kill him so that he doesn't spoil your happy ending."

"She turned me down." Marek let his hands drop to his sides and shrugged.

"Yes, I did," Annabel added, plucking up the

courage to rest her hand on Henry's arm. "Henry, Marek offered me marriage because he wanted to protect me from Zakonski. He is very kind but he is not in love with me." She wished she could continue, to speak to Henry of her love for him. But she could not.

"In that case I will fight Zakonski for myself then. If I win, Annabel, do I get the prize?"

She skipped a breath, heard her heart beat. His gaze locked hers. His darkened eyes tried to speak to her more words, she was sure, but what those words exactly were she could not be certain. What prize? She would give him anything he wanted.

"Yes," she murmured.

"I am staying out of this," Marek said backing away and turning to engage a group of young ladies.

"Yes, you do that," Henry muttered. "Annabel, will you dance with me?"

"With pleasure."

She took his arm and they glided forward into the drawing room where the musicians were getting ready to play.

"We open, my good people and the few bad ones who are also here, with a Polonaise," Szalynski announced.

Berekowski's daughter Ewa on the arm of the tall Count Weczlewski skipped into the middle of the room.

"Forget the duel, forget Zakonski, forget everything," Henry said so close to her ear she could feel his breath. "Think only of the music, and...if it pleases you, the man."

"It pleases me," she replied knowing she could not help smiling and that she would take his advice. This moment was to be lived for what it was.

"Let's dance," he said leading her forward.

The Polonaise, a stately, elegant dance, full of chivalry and pageantry, and yet with every step she yearned to be closer to him.

When the dance was finished, she thought he might leave her and it made her ache. "Will I see you later?" she asked. "Upstairs?"

"If you think it is not unwise..." Henry paused. "Is that a waltz the band is beginning? Annabel, will you? After all, I am already a marked man. What can one more dance do?"

Annabel swallowed. She let her hand fall away from his. He only had to say something, to declare himself, and there would be no duel.

"It is certainly a waltz." He slid his arm around her waist and feeling his warmth and maleness so close, and touching her so intimately, she could not resist.

They danced, the sweeping melody taking them from one corner of the room to the next while other couples danced around them.

"Do you know that in England, the waltz is regarded as somewhat scandalous," Henry said. "Though in many places it is now danced, but gentlemen have to be very careful how they hold their ladies."

"As close as this?"

"Never as close as this." And he pulled her even closer to him so that she felt the movement of his legs as they turned one way and then the other.

Though Henry's manner was often serious, there was a lightness to him that she enjoyed. He had a keen and intelligent sense of humor. He also made her stomach feel like jelly. If only he would kiss her again.

Of course that was impossible here.

"I shall see you later," she said and forced herself to walk away when the musicians brought the dance to a close. She'd dance with a number of other gentlemen and pretend that her heart was in it.

****

Henry left the drawing room when the dance had finished. He wanted something to drink. What he also wanted was not to have to watch her dancing with other men. Count Gronowski had come to claim her hand for the next dance immediately.

One part of him knew that he was behaving foolishly over this very woman he'd vowed to never allow to dictate his feelings to him. The rest of him would not allow him to stop. He wanted her, and now that she'd been married, and that so much time had passed, it was hardly wrong to pursue her with all the encouragement she had given him.

She had even told him that she'd turned down Marek's offer of marriage. He felt something like a pang in his chest. She probably enjoyed her independence as a widow.

"Henry!" Marek came across the hall and drew him slightly to one side. "I have spoken with Szalynski about your unfortunate engagement. We leave for Krakow at dawn."

"Why the rush?"

"We do not want our friend, the wolf, to get back to Krakow before us." Marek smiled lazily and waved his arm, looking for all the world as if he was retelling some hunting story. "And I want to keep him in our sights. I am going to hire a man to watch him. Don't worry, I know someone but he is in Krakow. And you must be careful, Henry. He is out to kill you and I would wager it won't be in this supposed duel."

"I am aware of that," Henry muttered.

"And when he is done with you," Marek continued, "he will find an excuse to call Szalynski to account. None of us doubt that."

"So are you planning to kill...the wolf, before I get my chance?" Henry asked.

"I am hoping it won't come to that. It is one

thing to know you have killed men on the battlefield but cold-blooded murder; I have never done that or intend to if I can help it. No, I want to find out if we can take the wolf out in another way. Discredit him. This is what I have been talking to Szalynski about for he knows more about Zakonski than any man here. It is why he invited him here in the first place. Szalynski is the kind of man who likes to keep his enemies close to him."

"How can he be discredited?"

"There are a number of possibilities but our time is short and I can do nothing while we are still here."

"We leave at dawn then." Henry inclined his head and then pressed his glass of wine to his lips and drank.

In the meantime he was being watched. Spied on by people just curious to have a detail they could add to the gossip, but also perhaps by a more sinister element. To that end he must appear as ordinary as possible. Perhaps he owed Countess Mielszenski a dance.

Henry knew as much as everyone else did that Zakonski's challenge was a sham. And if the rumor he heard was true that Zakonski, far from being a loyal Pole, supported the Austrian government of Galicia. There was a chance, just a chance that there was more to this than a family feud over some lands. Perhaps Szalynski, and maybe Marek, could answer that.

He turned to ask Marek something about it. Marek had gone.

Chapter Fifteen

Annabel heard the four sharp raps and sprang up at once, drew back the bolts from her door, and opened it less than a hand's span at first. She peered out.

"Henry," she whispered, seeing his steady countenance, the way the curls of his hair caught the taper lights of the corridor and shone burnished gold. She opened the door wide and he stepped quickly inside, pushed the door shut and bolted it.

"We must be careful," he said. Annabel thought his solid frame was worth more to her than a dozen bolts on her door. When he was with her all her fear seemed to flap its wings and was gone.

He drew her into his arms easily, wrapped his hands around her, and held her next to him. Words were not needed, she desired to simply feel him against her. Annabel breathed in what her nose told her was laundered wool, silk, sandalwood and another heady aroma. A scent very male and very luxurious, as rich perhaps as the perfume of an Arabian divan. She rested her head against his shoulder, tried to ignore the quickening of her heart as she felt his fingers at first touch, and then stroke her hair.

After some still, silent minutes where all she heard was the rise and fall of his chest, curiosity drew her to move back and gaze up. She wanted to see his expression. It was dark, fixed. There was a slight knot to his brow she wanted at once to reach up and smooth. He looked unhappy in a way she could not easily define.

How to cheer him?

Annabel took his gloved hand, pulled it up to meet her lips. Henry froze. Then he moved with a sudden force. He let his own hand drop and pulled at his dancing gloves, one after the other until his hands were free. He bent, laid his gloves carefully one on top of the other on top of the armoire that was nearby.

His naked fingers shone like porcelain, like his face also, in the fire light.

He took her hand in his, felt it, and kissed it. He did not let go, but held it fast. His eyes darkened further and he made no apology. He turned her hand in his own as delicately as a potter turns his clay. Henry began, in the half darkness, to undo the tiny buttons that fastened up her glove.

Three buttons. Four. Five. The feel of his naked fingers against her wrist sent little shivers all the way up her arm, to her mind, to her heart—enflamed it. Even her toes stretched, wakened.

Six. Seven. He peeled her glove easily from her hand, her fingers, dropping it on his own. He took each finger in turn, caressed it, and kissed it. Annabel thought she would melt and become a puddle on the floor.

He guided her hand under his evening coat, so that she felt the warm linen of his shirt, the top of his pantaloons where they met his waist. He left her hand there, holding on to him in a way that felt far too intimate to be comfortable yet at the same time completely right. He turned his attention to her other hand and inflicted the same treatment on it.

He drew the second hand into position to mirror the first. She had him, it seemed, in her grasp yet nothing prepared her for the tiny kisses he leant forward to place on her neck, her throat.

"Henry," she whispered, wanting to have some part of the gifts he was giving her.

"Annabel." He pulled back and regarded her. His forehead creased but his eyes burned. His breath was heavy. "Perhaps I should go?"

"No, don't go. Stay with me." The words came from somewhere.

He breathed deeply, continued to look at her, his eyes flickering in a way that made her aware he was thinking. Thinking, perhaps, too much. She knew what she wanted, she just wanted to feel.

"Bedtime?" he questioned.

Annabel took in sharp breath. If he meant...? No, he could not mean that. They were not husband and wife, after all—not even engaged.

He bent down, had scooped her into his strong arms before she could think or protest. Henry walked the three steps until he dropped her gently onto her bed.

"Oh, I am still dressed!" Annabel exclaimed. She knew her voice sounded girlish and wished it were not so.

He started to move, stopped. There was a sudden awkwardness as if someone had left the window open and a cold breeze had swept in.

"Do you want me to help?" He raised an eyebrow.

She pushed her hands down into the bed to push herself off it and to her feet. She would have to deal with things herself.

"Have you undressed many ladies?" she asked. Suddenly she wanted to know.

Henry watched her yet kicked his left foot into his right heel. His hand came forward and he rubbed it across his chin.

"Have you?"

"No," he said. A flush of shame and panic seared his face. He cast his eyes towards her window trying to hide it.

"I could call for my maid but then you would

have to leave...or you can undo the buttons on my back."

Henry stepped forward, the willing pupil.

Annabel turned her back to him. "Undo them, please, all the way to my waist."

He did as she asked. Her dress loosened, button by button.

"Thank you," she whispered. She removed her dress herself and placed it in the clothes press.

Never before had she been in a room like this with a man, dressed in her bodice and undergarments. Not even with her husband.

"Annabel, sweet Annabel," he said, interrupting her thoughts and sweeping her into his arms.

"Wait," she said. She was not sure what to say next, but a small pip of fear had risen inside her. Perhaps he did mean to...?

"Let me get this infernal thing off," he said and worked at the laces of her bodice.

She told herself firmly not to be scared. Yet she could hardly tell if the ripples that coursed through her as he untied her laces were thrills of fear or of anticipation.

Then he carried her, laid her on her bed, and pressed kisses on every exposed part of her. Annabel thought she would die with the pleasure of it. He kissed her face, her neck, her chest, and her breasts. She had never realized the sensations that such kisses could provoke.

"I shouldn't be here," he said rising up.

She reached up and caught his lips with her own, pulled him down so that his body laid on hers, pressing into her.

"Stay with me," she insisted as he again rose as if to leave her.

"I'll stay with you for a while." He tucked the blankets and counterpane over them and held her as if they were two spoons, scandalously close to one another. He planted a kiss at the nape of her neck.

"You are undoing me," he muttered. She was unsure what he meant.

Suddenly with a passion that seemed feral, he kissed her on the mouth and pressed hard against her, every muscle molding to hers. And while she thrilled at his deep plundering, she stiffened at the feel of his hand moving up the insides of her thighs to a place it should not go.

She jerked away.

She caught the puzzlement on his face as she moved along the bed and farther away from him.

He did not speak. Nor did she. What could she say? All she knew was that she had stopped something she very much feared, that her heart was racing and she felt a strange coldness from having pulled away from him.

"Forgive me," he said at last.

She could not reply. There was nothing to forgive. He had acted as any man would have. She was the one who was at fault.

Slowly he eased himself from the bed and tucked the blankets in where he had lain. He put his jacket and boots back on and left her without another word.

Too late now. Annabel huddled under the bedclothes. He did not know, and she could not explain. He'd had a childhood with a mother and a father whereas she had killed hers by being born. Her mother in childbed and her father from the grief. Lord Wells had not wished to see his only daughter, only child grow up. He had walked out of the house one day, not long after and out into a field and shot himself.

She had only been an infant, too young to have any memories of him. Yet it was enough to make her afraid of being close to anyone. She did not deserve a man like Henry, so certain of himself in the world.

****

Light pierced his consciousness even though Henry had yet to open his eyelids. Robards had hoisted the curtains back.

"Time to rise and shine, sir. Morning is just about broken."

Henry groaned. Like the sunlight, his memories of the night before flooded in. "I can see myself up."

Quarter of an hour later he was nearly up and dressed. While he regarded the fact that he had accepted an unwise duel with a degree of stoicism, what disturbed him more was how Annabel had led him on, and so far on, before making it clear she wanted none of his attentions. She might as well have slapped him in the face. Being humiliated by women was becoming a bit of a habit, he mused. Unfortunately, on this occasion he seemed overwhelmed by a feeling of sadness. He had thought that Annabel was more than a flirtation. She had even given him the idea that she cared for him, cared about his safety at least.

An almighty banging sounded in the corridor. Robards frowned but opened the door.

Marek burst in like a storm.

"He's gone. Zakonski's left for Krakow already. Come on, Henry, not a moment to lose."

****

Annabel woke and at once was assailed with the memory of a rather strange dream that Henry had been here. That she had been lying, undressed, in his arms.

No dream. She was still wearing her undergarments. Her dress and bodice? Where were they?

Helena walked in.

"Ah, you are awake, my lady. I have laid out your clothes."

Annabel jumped out of bed. Helena was probably looking at her strangely, for usually in bed

166

she wore a nightrail, but if she was intrigued or scandalized she said nothing.

Half an hour later Annabel was in the castle stables. She stood beside her stallion and rested her head on his warm, strong neck and smoothed her hand down his flank as the groom finished adjusting her saddle.

Henry walked into the stall. He wore an elegant black jacket and knee high boots but that didn't draw the eye as much as his fawn colored buckskins. These gave to any observer as accurate an impression of his legs from knee to mid thigh as if they were a bronze cast. Last night she had felt those very thighs next to her own. Her knees shook.

"Good morning, Annabel. Have I turned into a turnip?"

"No, I was just admiring your...outfit," she mumbled. "Good morning, Henry."

"Very average attire for a gentleman about to get on a horse."

Not average at all looking on you, she thought.

"Right, we need to get going." He slid one hand through his hair, a gesture that made her wonder if he was nervous. "Apparently Zakonski is already on the road. He has probably about an hour on us."

Annabel felt all the blood drain out of her body. She stumbled, thought she might faint, and gripped the harness. They would get to Krakow and Zakonski would try and kill Henry.

"Are you unwell?" Henry stepped forward.

"No." She waved her hand at him and told the groom to hurry. "I am quite all right. We must go."

He turned away.

"Henry." She stepped forward and touched his arm. "Will you...take care?"

"Of course," he said far too easily. And then he moved so that she could no longer rest her fingers on his forearm.

"Do I have your word," she pressed nonetheless, "as a gentleman?"

"I give you my word." He smiled and there was nothing she could do but mirror it in return.

"If anything happens to you—"

"Nothing will happen to—"

"If anything does happen to you..." Her voice trailed away.

"Time presses," he said and turned away. "We should go."

"Time presses," she echoed.

****

"I am setting the wheels in motion right away," Marek muttered as they dismounted in the courtyard of his house that afternoon. "I shall see you later."

Marek was, of course, referring to the investigations he wanted to undertake to see if he could bring Zakonski down. It was fortunate for Henry that Zakonski should be Marek's enemy as well as his own. If Marek's plan came off it would be a good thing, but he was not about to rely on anyone to get himself out of this apart from himself. He had to assume the worst.

Henry removed his cloak and hat, and passed them to the footman in the hall. He ran his hand along the banister as he bounded up the stairs. It was lucky that he was proficient at house breaking, he thought with a twisted smile, as that was exactly what he intended to do at Count Zakonski's residence tonight.

Then tomorrow, he would have to leave town. Gentlemanly honor be damned. He entered his chamber and closed his door behind him. He owed Jonathan Harvey dinner more than he owed Zakonski the pleasure of a duel. Besides the duel was a trap. *Better he that runs away and lives to fight another day*, he said to himself, looking in the mirror.

There was only one unsolved problem in his mind: Annabel.

How tomorrow panned out would depend entirely on tonight, he decided. A clever man is one who deals with things one at a time. First he was going to have a wash and get changed into evening dress exactly as if he was going out to dinner.

Half an hour later Henry stole up *Ulica Szpitalna*, dressed immaculately in his evening clothes. He wrinkled his nose at the scent of the sandalwood that Robards always insisted in dousing him in.

He had nearly gotten over it, when he had to stop and pause with his arm leaning on the frame of a doorway and sneeze.

He pulled out his handkerchief and blew his nose properly.

There was the front door of Annabel's house before him, lit with a single lantern. He could enter very easily but in the full knowledge of every servant and any spy who Zakonski had planted there. Or he entered the house unseen.

He wasn't going to make a very good house breaker if he kept sneezing. It seemed to have passed, the ticklishness. He wrinkled his nose one final time for good measure and was pleased to discover it had certainly passed.

He skirted down a nearby side street which he discovered he'd correctly surmised led to an entrance at the back of the house. This was where, he presumed, Annabel's carriage and horses were kept.

Then he saw it. Lying down on its side against the wall of one of the outbuildings was a long ladder. Henry smiled to himself. What a stroke of luck. The ladder looked to be at least ten to twelve feet long by his reckoning. He could easily get onto the roof of the outbuilding with it, and from there into the second floor window of the house just above it.

He picked up the ladder and propped it up against the outbuilding's wall and was on the roof in no time. He nearly slipped as a tile was loosened under his foot and crashed to the ground. He stilled but no one came to investigate the noise.

Henry pulled himself up so that he sat on the window ledge of the house. The curtains were drawn but the room inside was dark. He worked with his fingers to ease the casement. It was rather stiff but it was only a few minutes until he had jerked it free and was opening the window.

He climbed inside, careful to make only the smallest amount of sound. He straightened up and saw, in the dim light that filtered through from the open curtains, that he was in what appeared to be an empty bedchamber.

He tiptoed across the room and peered out into the corridor. It was dark, lit only at one end from what he could see. The stairs, he surmised, and edged out of the room and towards the light. Where was he going to find Annabel?

The light burned at the top of the staircase. Keeping to the shadows, Henry slowly descended to the first floor. He had his bearings now, and would see if she was to be found in her drawing room. He crept along to the double doors and paused, listened. Light came from the room and he could hear the crackle of the fire.

Slowly, ever so slowly, he turned the handle of the door, pushed it open by degrees until it was open about three inches and he could peer inside.

She sat by the fire with her back to the door, with something in her hand.

Needlework or reading, he supposed, for her head was bent in concentration.

He found himself following the curve of her neck, and then snatched his gaze away.

Now was not the time for such indulgences.

He opened the door farther and stepped into the room.

"Annabel. Good evening," he said quietly.

Chapter Sixteen

Annabel turned around and saw him. She dropped her needlework on the floor. "Henry! How on earth... Why did a servant not announce you?"

"I am fairly certain that none of your staff are aware I am here," he replied, shutting the door noiselessly behind him.

"Oh?" What was he doing here? How had he got in?

"I broke in and for that I apologize." He sounded very sincere. "There is no damage done, however."

"Henry? What—"

"Shhh!" He put a finger to his lips and came towards her. "It is better that no one knows I am here. I must speak with you urgently."

He knelt down in front of her and for a moment she could not think what he was doing. It came to her. Why else did a gentleman kneel at a lady's feet? There was no other reason. She trembled.

"Annabel," he said and picked up her hands in his. He wore gloves but they were kid gloves and very soft. Her hands were bare for she had been doing needlework, trying to take her mind off everything that had happened. He held her hands in his and seemed to be thoughtful. Perhaps he had not planned exactly what to say.

She waited and became aware of the ticks of the long case clock. She might as well consider what her answer would be now. She knew in her heart that she wanted to be his wife. Perhaps with his help she might overcome her fear of the other thing. It would not be many years before she was past the age for child bearing in any case.

"Will you come to London with me?" he said.

"Go with you to London?" What a strange question. Of course she would go. That was why he had come to Krakow in the first place so she had understood from her aunt and uncle.

He frowned. "Yes, come with me. To London. On Monday."

"Monday?" Annabel swallowed. "This is very...sudden."

"Yes, I leave on Monday," he replied, his gaze never wavering. His tone was matter-of-fact. It was cold. It made her uneasy. Was this his way of proposing that she should become his mistress?

Annabel stared into his dark, intense eyes. "Yes," she said, "but—"

"No time for discussions." He squeezed her fingers. "You must be packed and ready to go at eight o'clock on Monday morning. And tell no one. No one at all what you are doing or where you are going. Except your maid. She will come with you I take it?"

"Yes, Helena will come with me, but—"

"No buts." He placed her hands back in her lap. He rose, and leaned forward to kiss her forehead. She felt as if she had been stung there. So sweet that he kissed her and yet could he not bring himself to kiss her lips anymore? He turned towards the door. She wanted to ask him if Marek was coming with them but there were more important things she needed to ask. A moment ago she had thought he was about to propose marriage, now she was unsure exactly what he had proposed to her.

"Wait!" she said, rising to her feet. "I need to ask you..."

He stilled and nodded.

"Are you asking me to become your mistress?" There she had said it. Her heart thudded in her chest.

The moment he took to reply stretched out like a long, hot summer's coach ride. "I had not considered that such an arrangement would be to your liking. Indeed, you gave me every reason to think the opposite."

She did not know what to say.

"Until then," he said and slipped out of the room.

Eight o'clock, Monday morning. After the duel. He was going to fight the duel. Annabel felt her heart still with fear. She had to stop him.

****

Ulica Kanonicza was deathly quiet apart from the patter of the rain. Henry hurried, aware that in this heavy shower, his cloak, cut to face a ballroom rather than the elements, would not keep him dry for very long.

Watch a man play, Marek had said to him one evening in Vienna after he had won at the card table. Henry remembered how Marek had lowered his tone, as if imparting some grave secret, and he had drowned the dregs from his brandy glass and listened. *Watch a man play, lose a little if that is what it takes to buy you the time. Watch until you learn the man's weak spot. Then you will know what you have to do to win the game. Do nothing until you strike, and when you strike, strike to win.*

Henry jumped over a large puddle. The water was coursing down the street in rivulets now. Marek had been talking about cards, but Henry had seen at once their application to life in general, his own way of living in particular.

Zakonski's weak spot was his own self-interest. Henry had, strapped in a pouch under his jacket, gold and a thick wad of roubles. Worth more to Zakonski, he suspected, than his own miserable life.

Thunder crashed overhead and then the street

was suddenly illuminated in a stroke of lightning. Good, it would be much easier to break into Zakonski's house with the storm. He could break a window if he liked and no one would notice.

It didn't come to that as Henry found the back gate slightly ajar, and even more surprisingly, a back door that led into the servants' quarters. It must be supper time for there were no servants around. He slipped into the cold vestibule and followed the corridor as it turned towards the main part of the house.

He froze as he heard voices coming towards him. He had to take the chance and he opened a door to his right. It was a large pantry and he slipped inside thankfully. Unless it was servants coming to raid the larder...

The two people passed by. After a minute, Henry ventured out and continued until he came to the end of the corridor where there was a set of stairs that led upwards. Into the main house, he presumed, and took the stairs noiselessly, listening all the time in case he should hear anyone coming his way.

At the top of the stairs was a large black door. He opened it slowly, and hearing nothing, emerged into what was Zakonski's main hallway. He'd been here before. Now, he wanted to find the man himself, but first, he needed to go upstairs.

He climbed the main staircase quickly and couldn't quite believe he had got this far, this easily. Now where might the man Marek called "the wolf" have his study? Henry started to open door after door. Four doors later, he found it. It was unlocked and empty. Henry cursed his good luck and darted into the large room that overlooked the courtyard at the back of the house. It was lined with bookshelves and in the middle, a large desk.

He went straight over to the desk, ignored the

papers that lay strewn across it and tried the top drawer. It was locked.

"Henry!"

Henry turned around, his hand shooting under his jacket and to his pistol. Marek emerged from behind the curtain. "What the devil!"

"I could say the same to you, friend," Marek whispered in reply. "I'm here looking for evidence to bring him down."

"Found anything?"

Marek opened the left hand side of his jacket where Henry could see a number of papers stuffed therein.

"I've got enough to bring him down a hundred times over." Marek grinned. "He'll have so many enemies after this lot gets out and everyone realizes how they have been swindled and double-crossed, he'll never dare set foot in Krakow again. And with any luck someone will feel strongly enough about it and have him taken to court."

"What about this drawer?" Henry tapped the locked drawer in the desk.

"Couldn't get it open."

Henry knelt down and pulled some wires from a pocket inside his jacket.

"Oh, so you can pick locks?" Marek observed. Henry ignored the note of interest in his voice. "Forgive me asking, Henry, but sometimes I wonder if you are as innocent as you look?"

"I'm not that innocent," Henry agreed. He'd got one wire turning the mechanism and it would only take getting this second one right and the lock was his.

They heard footsteps outside in the corridor.

"Damn," Henry swore under his breath and pulled the wires out of the lock.

"Behind the curtain," Marek whispered.

They were hidden on the wide window ledge as

they heard the door handle being turned.

Two men entered the room and Henry was surprised to hear them speak to one another in Austrian German.

One voice sounded familiar, and then one of the men addressed his colleague by name and Henry knew why. Hantenberg. The Austrian he had met at Annabel's reception. A man Marek had called a devil.

From the shuffling of papers and the conversation, it was clear that the two Austrians were there for nearly the same purpose as them, to search the room. Except they were looking for some very particular papers. Something so important, Henry gathered that they must get it back into their own possession.

They also found the top drawer locked. Henry heard them rattle the drawer handle angrily.

After about ten minutes or so they seemed to give up and leave the room. Henry breathed a sigh of relief but something was wrong. They had not exactly been quiet in their search had they? Henry parted the curtains and stepped down from the ledge back into the room and wondered what was going on.

"Where's Zakonski?" he asked Marek.

"Out. I saw him leave on his horse and thought I'd come in."

More footsteps outside. Quieter footsteps. Henry cursed silently at himself as they darted back to their hiding place. Footsteps so quiet and his mind had been so busy they had almost missed them.

Two more men entered the room. Different men, who spoke in voices so low it was barely a whisper. Henry strained to try and hear what they were saying. Papers rustled. Was everyone in this city after Zakonski's papers tonight?

Then he heard one of the voices clearly. No man. A woman's voice, speaking in Polish. He recognized it. Annabel.

Without hesitation Henry flung back the curtain and completely ignored her gasp of surprise and the squeak that came from the maid.

"What on earth are you doing here?" he growled under his breath, seizing her hands as it occurred to him that she might do something foolish. It wasn't safe. "Have you gone mad?"

"Let go of me," she protested, but quietly. "I am here to get some papers. Land papers. My husband's estates. I must have them. Have you seen them?"

"I don't think I did." Marek frowned and began to rummage through the large pile of papers on the left-hand side of the desk.

"We've got to get you out of here. At once," Henry said. "How did you get in?"

"Helena, my maid, her cousin works here. She smuggled us in. I'm not going anywhere until I get those papers. What are *you* doing here?"

"It's not important." Henry frowned but let her hands go.

She immediately seized on the other pile of papers on the desk and started to rifle through them.

How he ached to bundle her over his shoulder and take her right out of here, there and then. Henry buttoned down his anger, his fear. He fumbled around in his pockets where he had stuffed his wires. Back to the drawer. Who knew what would turn up inside it? The sooner he found out, the sooner he was getting them all out of there. His plan to confront Zakonski in a little tête-à-tête would have to go right out the window.

"Look," the maid said. She had moved over to the glass and was looking out.

Henry turned his attention back to the lock. He got the first wire in place again easily. Now back to trial and error to find out what he had to do with the second.

The maid said something in Polish and Henry saw Marck's legs out of the corner of his eye move towards the window. Henry moved his ear closer to the drawer lock, listening for a tiny click.

And then he heard it. A final twist of the second wire exactly where he held it and the lock was open. Henry pulled the drawer open and emptied its contents onto the floor. Time was of the essence. There were a number of papers, or more properly he should say vellum, tied in bundles that looked as if they could be important.

"Annabel, come and look at these," he said. Some of the documents were in Polish and he hadn't a hope of deciphering whether or not they were significant.

"Henry," Marek said. "You might want to have a look at this."

"What?" Henry snapped, couldn't for a moment imagine what might be happening on the street outside to be of any interest except... "Is Zakonski home?"

"Yes."

Henry jumped to his feet and darted over to see. Zakonski was in the middle of his courtyard, still mounted on his horse. Opposite him stood Hantenberg and another man—a burly man he recognized at once as being one of the footpads! A groom or some other servant cowered in the corner. Hantenberg brandished a pistol.

Crash! A loud clap of thunder made Henry jump but did nothing, it seemed, to alter the scene below. There was a conversation, an argument, going on between Hantenberg and Zakonski.

"We're getting out of here," Henry said. His hand had already slid under his jacket of its own accord ready to draw his pistol.

"What? Out the back?" Marek gave an uneasy

laugh.

"No, we should be okay just to wander out the front door I think. Just as if we were supposed to be here." Henry snatched his hand back, listened. He could hear nothing from the corridor outside. Chances were they could make a dash for it now.

"Wait," Annabel said. "I need my papers."

"We can't wait." He would throw her over his shoulder in a minute and to the devil with the consequences.

"Got them! I think. Let me just check they are all here."

The room was cast deathly white. Henry stared out the window as a bolt of lightning came down from the darkness like the hand of God.

Zakonski's horse reared. He tumbled forward and slid heavily to the ground.

The horse appeared frantic but unhurt. It raised its head, its forelegs, whinnied hellishly and backed away. It took some moments before the groom dared to rush forward and try to calm it.

The maid's hand shot to her mouth as she stifled a gasp. She crossed herself in the Catholic manner. Marek exclaimed something in Polish that sounded like a curse.

Zakonski's fate was less certain. He laid, a stiff outstretched heap, on the ground below.

A swarm of servants, who must have been watching the scene, appeared. Hantenberg had put his pistol away. There was shouting and Zakonski moved.

"He is not dead," Marek said. "More is the pity."

Henry turned around.

"Annabel?" She looked up from where she was still kneeling on the floor, and paused shuffling through the papers in her hands. "Count Zakonski has been injured. He is here. We must go."

"What?" Annabel gripped the papers she held.

"Quickly." He reached forward and took her hand.

"Bolt of lightning frightened his horse and he fell. Well, he has worse coming." Marek pulled the papers he had taken out from inside his jacket and started to throw them on the fire.

"What are you doing?" Annabel cried and ran over to Marek.

"Poland has enough enemies as it is," Marek said, putting his hand out to stop her. "Zakonski will be stopped but this is not the way. It is better that he dies a loyal Pole than we inflict more pain into the people's hearts by telling them they had another traitor in their very midst."

Annabel stilled. "Perhaps you are right. But does Hen—, does Mr. Champion still have to—?"

"Come on. Let's go, shall we?" Henry's immediate concern was not Zakonski but Hantenberg and the footpad outside. It looked exactly to Henry as if Zakonski had been in Hantenberg's employ, and, true to form, had double-crossed him.

Henry darted over to the door, listened, opened it a fraction, and listened again. Silence. Everyone would be in the courtyard out the back. They could walk right out.

"Come on, quick!" he said. "Before there is hell to pay."

They walked straight out of the house as if they had been there for dinner, two gentlemen and two ladies—although one of the ladies' cloaks was somewhat on the shabby side. Henry grinned as he shut Zakonski's front door behind them.

"Take my arm," he commanded Annabel, bounding down the steps and leaving the maid to Marek's care. She obeyed and they walked at the fastest speed possible without drawing undue attention to themselves.

Once they had reached the top of *Ulica Kanonicza* Henry felt safer.

"Did you get the papers you wanted?" he asked Annabel.

"Yes," she replied and said nothing further.

Once they had crossed the *Rynek Glowny* and were heading towards the small market square at the foot of *Ulica Szpitalna*, Henry felt safer still. They had certainly not been followed.

"Do not forget we go early on Monday," he whispered to her. "Eight o'clock."

"We still leave Krakow on Monday? Why not tomorrow?" Her eyes widened. "But Za—"

"I have a rendezvous at dawn on Monday. You know that."

"No! You mustn't—"

"Shhh!" he said silencing her. Bells and whistles! She wasn't going to change her mind now, was she? He wasn't having it. Marek and he had agreed they were going on Monday as soon as the dreadful business was over, and she was coming with him if he had to drag her. He wanted to take her hands, to draw her into his arms, comfort her, protect her, and whisper nonsense into her ear to make her understand that he loved her.

He loved her.

The sudden realization of that fact should also have sent him reeling. He pushed his weight back on his heels, rocked forward. That was all he allowed himself.

Her agreeing to go to London with him had nothing to do with himself after all. He was just a servant in all this, a means to achieve a goal. "You will be happy in London, with your family there," he said.

****

Early on Sunday morning, before the bells of St. Mary's had even begun to peal for the first mass,

Annabel drew her own curtains. She immediately began to dress.

"Helena, where are you?" she muttered under her breath. She had especially told her maid to be with her early.

Helena arrived in time to help her lace up her stays. She often did not wear stays but today she would be riding.

"Where are we going? Can I ask this?" Helena said.

"Castle Szalynski."

"We have only just been there!"

"We go there again. I must see the count. It is urgent. Tomorrow, as you know, we leave for England." If Henry was still alive by then. Annabel closed her eyes for a moment and drew a long breath as Helena pulled her ribbons for the final time. She had stopped herself fainting or weeping or doing anything else she suddenly felt like acting out of character and doing. She had the land papers. She must take them to the count and hope... and pray.

Chapter Seventeen

They had ridden through the breaking dawn to
Balice Forest on the edge of the city. It was misty
and cold and Henry was glad he'd accepted the thick
wool cloak Marek had offered him for the ride.

"Here is the spot." Marek drew to a halt just
before a clearing. "We'll tie the horses here."

Henry dismounted, his boots landing on the
ground with a crunch. He tethered his mount beside
Marek's and looked about him. There was nobody
else in sight. He pulled out his watch and flipped it
open. They were quite early. He said, "I'm pleased
you know your way around this forest."

"Extensive, isn't it?" Marek dusted off his cuffs
and strode ahead towards the clearing. "Even the
Swedes couldn't raze it in 1655 though they
destroyed Balice village. The palace is rebuilt in the
Italian style by a certain heiress, Urszula
Darowska." Marek flashed a grin. "But we will not
disturb her sleep from here."

"This clearing has been used for duels before?"

"Frequently."

Henry wondered whose blood he might be
treading on. A prickle of unease tickled the back of
his neck.

"Dueling is such a foolish business," Marek said
as he paced out the ground. "But a clever fool does
his groundwork, eh, Henry?"

Henry was unable to laugh or make a remark
back. Shortly after dawn someone was going to die
and there remained the tiniest fear in his chest that
the gentleman in question could be him. He

shivered, as if, as they say, someone had walked over his grave. *Henry Edmund Champion. Born 1784. Died 1817 in unfortunate circumstances overseas. Rest in Peace.*

No, he had too much to do back in England. He had decided. His life must have a purpose and he must do everything he could to try and get into Parliament. He'd strive to change some of the cruelties his fellow men inflicted on those unable to represent themselves.

No doubt it would be easier to be a man of less honor. He could have escaped to England yesterday, not stayed here to fight a duel with a man who apparently had no honor. You will slay him with your honor, Marek had said. In the end, honor always triumphs. Did it? Did evil not triumph sometimes?

The snap of a twig pierced his reverie and Henry looked up. Zakonski, followed by a man he did not recognize, walked towards them.

"Here early I see," Zakonski said. "May I present Pan Grzegorz Radoczill, my second."

Radoczill seemed to shake hands begrudgingly. He had an ugly scar across his forehead and looked more like a footpad than a gentleman. Henry wondered if he had indeed been one of the footpads who had accosted him that evening when they had first gone to see Countess Szalynski. He pushed Annabel's memory quickly from his mind. He did not want to think about her now.

"Would you like to inspect the ground yourself, before we start?" Marek said to Zakonski.

"Certainly." Zakonski and his henchman went off to pace the clearing for themselves.

"A pleasant pair," Marek remarked in a low voice. "Keep an eye on them. They appear to have come alone but we don't want any surprises. I am going to check where their horses are and that we really are alone."

Marek departed. Alone? Yes, he felt alone, but with two enemies only yards away. Henry tried to slow his breathing. It was too fast. The dark-leaved boughs of the forest were closing in on him.

He shook himself. He had to remain calm. He was imagining things.

Marek returned a few moments later. "Their horses are tethered close to ours. Everything seems in order. I can't see any evidence of anyone else being here but we must remain on our guard."

"Yes."

"How are you feeling Henry? You look a little pale."

"I am not looking forward to this."

"You know what to do, simply shoot him in the arm, his pistol arm of course. Wound him. Then honor is preserved."

"And if he is quicker than me?"

"He won't be as we intend to cheat, remember. You must turn around just before the counting is over as we agreed. When I say nineteen. Bang." Marek smiled. "We go home for a hunter's breakfast."

And if Zakonski cheats? Henry kept that thought to himself. He was a good shot, he knew that. He was sure he could get the pistol arm from forty paces if he had a moment to concentrate and aim. But did he have that moment? Their plan was hardly foolproof.

"Time to begin, gentlemen, I believe." Zakonski called over to them. "You have brought the pistols, Ralenski, have you not? I should like to inspect them."

"Of course, and you may pick first, as agreed." Marek opened his bag and took out the small rosewood box of dueling pistols. "They were my fathers," he remarked.

Henry began to grow irritated. This was no time for nostalgia.

Marek held the box open as Zakonski picked up each pistol in turn and inspected it. At last he made his decision and Henry withdrew the remaining pistol. A thought suddenly occurred to him. He had not inspected both pistols. Could he really trust that Marek had not tampered with anything? Of course he could. Marek would not betray him to Zakonski. His hands trembled as he loaded the pistol with powder. The niggling doubt would not go away.

Not even as they turned their backs on one another and Marek began the count. "One...two...three..."

One foot in front of the other—as though he was a clockwork figure wound up for the amusement of a child. Henry tightened his grip on the pistol.

"Nine... Ten... Eleven..."

He checked again that the pistol was fully cocked and felt his finger trembling against the trigger.

"Wait! Halt! Stop! *Zostaw!*"

The voice was so commanding that Marek fell silent. Henry stood completely still, uncertain what was happening and afraid to turn around.

"Stop! The duel cannot go ahead."

"I have stopped counting," Marek said. "Count Zakonski, Mr. Champion, the duel is suspended. Please disarm yourselves and turn around. A gentleman has arrived with some news."

"What gentleman?" Zakonski growled. "Oh, it is you, Szalynski."

Henry turned around but did not immediately return his pistol to half-cock. He held it pointing to the ground and regarded Count Szalynski as he dismounted from a tall, black stallion. He kept the corner of his eye fastened on Zakonski, but Zakonski stood still where he was, also watching Szalynski.

Through the quiet came the sound of every scrape of his boots as Szalynski tethered his horse.

"Thank you for your patience, gentlemen," he said, facing them at last.

Henry felt his pulse quicken again.

"I have a proclamation." Szalynski opened a packet that hung about his neck and withdraw a scroll which he unfurled dramatically. "Dueling on Mondays is hereby forbidden in Balice Forest by order of—"

"No, you don't!" Zakonski shook his head vigorously. "Always the theatrical one, Szalynski, but you won't play that trick with me. This duel was arranged fair and square, at your castle, with your guests as witnesses. It will go ahead this morning."

"Zakonski, I heard you had been injured. A fall from a horse? Your sword arm has been a little painful?"

"You are well informed." Zakonski's eyes narrowed.

"Hardly fair to proceed when one party is injured. I think you will find it is all for the best not to fight this morning. Gentlemen?"

Zakonski reached into his coat but before he had time to retrieve his arm, a loud crack and pistol powder exploded into the air. Zakonski fell backwards in silence. No time to cry out. He hit the forest floor with a thump.

It happened so fast, yet Henry seemed to witness it as if time had slowed down.

Szalynski held his pistol pointing towards the ground while it cooled. "If only he had conquered his temper," he said, "it would not have come to this."

"I did not think it would coome to this," Marek echoed.

Henry was silent, absorbing Zakonski's death and Szalynski's sudden action.

Radoczill said something in Polish that sounded

like a question and was answered rapidly by Szalynski. An intense dialogue between them followed. Henry tried to interpret Rodoczill from the way he held himself and his gestures but could not discern much. Eventually Radoczill bowed his head to Szalynski and moved away to where Zakonski's body lay.

"I am sorry to deny you the pleasure, Mr. Champion," Szalynski said. "But the revenge was mine to have. He killed my brother."

Marek came forward and patted Szalynski on the back. "I shall see that a good report circulates."

"But..." Henry began. He did not quite understand.

"Henry, are you blind? The deceased clearly died of a pistol wound and no doctor of sane mind will say otherwise."

"You will say that I killed him?"

"Duels happen, Mr. Champion, and if the affair is conducted with honor, then so be it. Radoczill will not say anything to the contrary. He is to receive a small sum of money for his trouble in removing and reporting the body."

"I see."

"You will be in England in any case. And you will not actually have his death on your conscience," Szalynski finished.

"Of course. Thank you. I am indebted to you."

Szalynski shook his head. "No, no. It is I who am indebted to you, Mr. Champion. Besides, you are our guest here in Poland. It was quite wrong of me to allow you to agree to a duel with Zakonski in the first place. I should have stood up at the castle and taken him on myself. And you are to marry my sister, are you not? She deserves to be happy."

Henry finally put his pistol back to half-cock. "If she will have me," he muttered, surprised that Szalynski had guessed his intentions.

"I am not in any doubt," Szalynski said. "Now, shall we return to the city? Ralenski, I trust you have thought to tell your servants to lay on a good breakfast?"

"A good breakfast, yes." Marek yawned. "For we intend to leave for England in a couple of hours."

****

Bells sounded the hour at eight o'clock on Monday morning, sending pigeons flapping into a maelstrom around the city spires. Standing outside the front of her house, Annabel said her own silent farewell, for now, to the city she had lived in these last nine years and to Szalynski who had appeared in time for her departure. She could not describe her relief when he had arrived not quarter of an hour ago to tell her that Zakonski was dead, and more importantly, that Henry was alive.

She turned to follow Helena into the carriage. Henry and Marek had arrived and now a whole new chapter of her life was beginning.

She looked out of the window at Henry. His face was like stone. Hard and angular and she didn't understand why. She watched him pull at the bit of his hired mount.

"Are you ready?" he asked.

"Yes, ready." She wondered why it was so that the words, so innocent in themselves, threatened to choke her. There were tears at the back of her eyes she had denied the existence of until now. She told herself she must be strong. In her dreams Henry would have helped her into the carriage, kissed her hand, promised that he would see them safely to their destination. In her dreams he would have asked for her hand in marriage when he'd gone on bended knee before her last night.

So much for dreams. She once thought she had the power to map her own destiny by her own actions. How very naïve she had been. How very wrong.

"So, we go," she said. Henry was not even looking at her.

"To London!" Marek said rising to the sense of occasion by clicking his heels and waving his hand onwards with a flourish.

Henry watched him. Not a flicker passed his countenance. Nothing, she noticed, was in his expression except casual indifference. He pulled at his reins and turned his animal towards the road.

Annabel did not look out of the window again until they had left the city and traveled on a road flanked with meadows on either side. She leaned out of the window for the final time and looked towards the walled city with its roofs and towers. It presented a picture that an artist would be proud to capture. She would capture it, in her mind. Krakow must have looked as it did now for hundreds of years, before the Tartars had ridden over the plains, at the behest of Genghis Khan, laid waste to everything in their wake.

Yet Krakow had survived.

She would survive. They would survive. Now Zakonski was dead it was unlikely that anyone else would challenge the Szalynski lands. Her husband's family would get their rightful inheritance.

"It will be a long journey to England," she said to Helena. "Thank you for agreeing to come with me."

"A chance to travel to a foreign country, it is something special." Helena folded her arms. "I shall be happy in England and so shall you, my lady. It is time for both of us to move on."

Annabel wished she could share Helena's confidence. She knew she would be content enough to live in England again, but *happy*? That was something she could not imagine unless she could be with Henry. She glanced out of the window but he and Marek must be riding ahead.

****

"We've broken the back of the journey," Henry said leaning back in the comfortable horsehair chair. He twirled his wine glass between his fingers and then raised it. "Here's to Rheims, the home of Champagne, and the fine wines we have enjoyed this evening."

"And had a splendid dinner!" Marek raised his glass in return. "All this gilded furniture and rich fabrics," he looked about the hotel sitting room, "makes me nostalgic for Paris."

"Paris? No, thank you!" Henry slammed his glass back down on the table. "We're straight to Calais from here and on the packet boat before you can say Jack Robinson!"

"You have grown very sober in your old age, my friend. But anyway, here's to Merry England then." Marek raised his glass and then took a sip so large he titled his head back. "Ah! I look forward to it. Tell me, Henry, what are the ladies in London like?"

"They will love you, don't worry. You are a count and you have plenty of money, don't you? Just stay dashing and charismatic as you always are with the female sex and you will see they will respond just the same."

"I had heard that English girls were rather...reserved."

"Yes, they are. And heavily chaperoned. But I am sure you will rise to the challenge."

Marek took a long draught of his wine and set the glass down on the side table. "And what about you, Henry? What are your plans when we get to England?"

"I hadn't thought it out in detail to be honest. We should stay a while in London so you can see the sights but the season is coming to an end and everyone will be off to the country. It had crossed my mind we might go up to Leicestershire, if a hunting box can be found this late in the day. The hunting there is very good."

"Excellent!" Marek rubbed his hands together. "Henry, you are already shaping up to be a good host."

"And I must open up my own house," Henry continued. "That assumes that I will be able to purchase it back. It had to be sold to pay the creditors. Otherwise I shall be in the market for a small country estate no more than a day's ride from London."

"And what do you do with Annabel Szalynski?"

"Do? Why, deliver her directly to her relatives, Lord and Lady Roseley when we arrive in London."

"You know you have ignored her this whole journey?" Marek's eyes narrowed and Henry shifted in his seat. This change in conversation made him uncomfortable. "You have not spoken to her beyond what is a necessary and polite discourse. And now she retires every evening as soon as she can escape from dinner."

"You don't know what you are talking about."

"I know what I see!" Marek thumped his fist on the arm of his chair. "At the castle the two of you were like love birds! Henry, I like the woman and would marry her myself if she would have me but she values her independence too highly to marry for convenience."

Henry supposed that to be true. Married at a very young age and then suddenly widowed with no close relatives to look out for her. She must have become used to running her own affairs and ordering her life to her own satisfaction.

"She will marry, I would wager, if it is for love." Marek took a gulp of his wine so that the glass was dredged. "I have never been in love. What is it like?"

"You can have no idea until it hits you." Henry

193

smiled, unable to help himself. "And then, when it hits you, you know. You might confuse it at first with desire or lust but you find that that is only the tip of the iceberg. It is like being given something you always wanted, even if you never knew you wanted it, and you must have it. It fills your waking thoughts, torments you through the day. Like a canker growing in your body you cannot remove."

"And the cure?"

"I don't know what the cure is."

"For heaven's sake, Henry, ask Annabel to marry you and put us all out of our misery."

If only it was that straightforward. Something like a lead weight settled in the pit of Henry's stomach. She had kissed him and looked at him in ways he could only imagine; but there seemed to be nothing tangible. She had been polite enough to him throughout the journey but she seemed to prefer to keep company with her maid. Once or twice he had thought he'd seen something in her eyes inviting him to come closer, to talk to her intimately as they had done in Poland. But something held him back from responding. He could not precisely put a finger on what it was. Shyness? Awkwardness? A feeling that he simply wasn't good enough to become the husband of Countess Szalynski, formerly the Honorable Miss Annabel Wells.

Chapter Eighteen

Annabel imagined, when they landed at Dover and she was at last home on English soil, that her anxieties would diminish. They did not. In fact they seemed to grow and prosper each mile they drew nearer to London, and the inevitable moment when she would be parted from Henry.

She had heard him talk to Marek about business he had to see to regarding his affairs, and going up to Leicestershire for hunting. It did not seem likely that he would linger long in London. She did not think he had a house or rooms in the capital.

"It is not far to London now," she said to Helena as they stopped at a toll house. "Two or three hours I think, no longer."

"Are you excited?" Helena asked.

"Yes." She was looking forward to seeing Lord and Lady Roseley and catching up, she hoped, with many old friends with whom she had lost contact over the years.

The carriage jolted as they set off once more.

"Oh!" she gasped.

"Are you feeling all right?" Helena leaned forward and looked at her closely.

"Quite all right. My mind was somewhere else."

Annabel bit her lip. Her nerves were so tightly strung, like an over-wound violin, that the slightest thing disturbed her. Only two or three hours. And then...?

****

"Thank you, thank you." Roseley shut the door to the library behind them and clapped Henry on the

195

back. "You don't know what this means to me, to my wife, to have our dear niece here safely."

"Pleased to be of service, sir," Henry replied evenly, wondering what was coming next. An awkward discussion about money he did not doubt. He had done what Roseley asked and he would accept a modest fee. He would have liked to be simply the gallant but he could not afford to be too proud after losing his inheritance through his own stupidity.

"She thought she would be safe in Krakow when we heard that the city was to become a free city under the terms of the Treaty of Vienna," Roseley said. "Had Szalynski himself been alive and they had been in Warsaw they would of course at once have had to flee. You know the late Count Szalynski was a Polish patriot and strong supporter of Napoleon? And close friends with Prince Czartoryski?"

"Yes, I knew something of it," Henry replied. In truth he hadn't realized the whole. Annabel had been in more danger than even he had credited. Not just Zakonski but perhaps also from the Russians. The thought of it made his blood run cold. He quickly reminded himself she was here safely now, sitting upstairs at this very moment in the drawing room and drinking tea with her aunt.

"In short, we cannot thank you enough." Roseley reached down and opened the drawer of his desk and pulled out a clean sheet of writing paper. He put it on the desk facing Henry, and just to the right of it he placed a pen and ink well. "Now, young man, if you will be so good as to provide me here with the details of your bankers in London I shall arrange a suitable recompense. Shall we say ten thousand pounds? I'll have it transferred to your funds without delay. And then let us hear no more on the matter as if it never happened."

"Ten thousand pounds?" Henry could not help laughing. "My lord, I should have gladly brought your charge to England for nothing. But, through my own reduced circumstances and the expenses I have had to endure, I will gladly and gratefully accept a thousand."

"Eh?" Roseley frowned. "Noble words, but ten thousand pounds is not a sum to be laughed at. Why, it is enough to invest and provide you with an income for life."

"I am a gentleman—"

"Even so, take the money."

"Having now completed my European...travels, I intend to settle in England and pursue a career in Parliament. If..."

Roseley raised his eyebrows. "If you are seeking a sponsor, young man, that is something we can talk about further. But it does not absolve you from receipt of these ten thousand pounds. If you intend to be in Parliament, you will need a reliable income all the more."

Henry swallowed. "Thank you." He would be able to purchase a modest property now. If not all his family estate, then the house at least, and home farm with enough land. And still have money to invest for a modest income.

"You will want to say goodbye to my niece?" Roseley said when they had finished the paperwork.

"Yes, of course, thank you." He did not want to say goodbye to her at all but what other choice was there?

****

"Henry!" Jane Adams raced though the hallway of her Highgate house towards him. She ignored her butler who had stepped forward to relieve him of his coat, and flung herself at him. "Aren't you pleased to see your one and only sister again? After all this time?"

"Of course I am," he replied, holding her gingerly and planting a kiss on the top of her head. He had been shocked, that was all, to see the swell around her middle. She was quite clearly with child. His third niece or nephew was on the way, while he remained steadfastly a bachelor. "It is just, well, you look so...grown up!"

"Oh, dear!" Jane said pulling herself off him as she realized, Henry presumed, that she'd also ignored the gentleman standing beside him. "Henry, your guest?"

"May I present Count Marek Ralenski."

"Madam, your servant." Marek kissed his sister's hand with his typical flourish.

"Count Ralenski, how delightful to meet you and have you as our guest here in Highgate. Though we are not in town itself, it is only a short ride to London and very convenient. You must with all speed make yourself at home. Hill will show you about the house and your rooms and then we will take tea in the drawing room. Now, will you excuse me while I steal Henry away for a few minutes to meet his nephew and niece?"

"Certainly." Marek gave a little bow.

"Come on, brother," Jane said, fingering the banister impatiently. "I have been telling Thomas and Caroline all about Uncle Henry and his adventures; so don't be surprised if you get lots of questions, from Thomas anyway. He does not remember you from before, but he is nearly three and a half years old now and becoming very curious. And I want to hear, of course, everything you have been up to."

She waited, just long enough for him to remove his coat, before leading him upstairs to the nursery.

"Thomas, this is your Uncle Henry," Jane said taking the small boy's hand from his nurse's and leading him over.

Henry crouched on the ground and picked up one of the tin soldiers that lay on the floor, though found his mind was in another place: Krakow. He recovered himself quickly. "Hello, Thomas. Is this one of your soldiers?"

"No," Thomas shook his head, "it's a Frenchie."

"So where are the English redcoats?"

"Put away." Thomas pointed to a box of jumble.

"Resting in their barracks I see," Henry said. "We'll have to wake them later, you know, if there are Frenchies about."

Henry watched Thomas's eyes sparkle with possibilities he could not yet articulate.

"Where's Caroline?" Jane asked the nurse.

"Asleep, madam. Next door."

Jane handed Thomas back into the care of his nurse and motioned to Henry to follow. She placed a finger on her lips. "You can just take a peek," she whispered.

Caroline had hair exactly the dark brown color of her father, lying in curls that framed a cherubic face.

"Caroline will break lots of hearts," Henry said once they had shut the door and were back in the corridor. "And Thomas is a fine lad." He was envious of his brother-in-law in this respect, that much he would admit.

"Thank you, Henry. I knew you would love them. Just wait until you have children of your own. You were so good with Thomas I wondered if you had been practicing!"

"Certainly not," he replied with some indignation in his voice. "There's plenty of time for all that. Is Thomas the elder at home?" He had better steer the conversation elsewhere. His chest felt rather tight and he needed to sit down, preferably with a large glass of brandy in front of him—no, the whole decanter. He wanted lots of daughters, just like Annabel.

"Thomas is in the House today. There is an important debate. About corn. I think he intends to speak."

"Ah, yes. I would speak with him about that. I was thinking about going into Parliament myself and I may have even found myself a sponsor."

"Really? Oh, Henry, does that mean you might stay in England? For a while?"

"I might stay a good while," he replied.

"Henry, you don't know how happy that makes me. Will you live here in London or do you intend to return to Sevenoaks?"

"Both, if I can manage it. And, if it is possible, I intend to buy our house back."

"Henry! How wonderful!" Jane clapped her hands together. "Ours was such a beautiful house and so sad that it is the property of another family. It should be full of your children running around and causing havoc. Henry, you must marry!"

"One step at a time, sister." Did women have nothing else in their confounded heads but marriage and nurseries?

"Oh, dear! I have said something I should not. I can see from the way your eyes have clouded over that it was the wrong subject to propose. Is there a lady, Henry? What is it? Does she not wish to marry you?"

"I don't know. I have not asked her."

"I knew it! Why ever not? You should ask her."

"You don't know anything about the situation!"

"I can see that you are in love with her, most terribly. You must ask her, Henry. I will warrant that if she sees the expression in your face that I just did, she will not be able to resist you. And besides, you are a handsome devil and rather fun when you forget to be serious."

"Let's see how Count Ralenski is settling in."

Henry could not bring himself to speak to his sister about Annabel, yet. His feelings were too strong and they threatened to bubble to the surface and shatter his command of himself. "I believe you asked for tea to be served in the drawing room?"

****

London was so terribly regular, Annabel considered. The roads were wide. Everywhere she looked there was symmetry, pattern, order. Each brick seemed to be perfectly aligned with its neighbor. Every decoration had a reflection. On Lady Roseley's mantlepiece the ornaments all came in pairs: two small china vases that looked like Roman amphora, two creamware candlesticks, a pastoral shepherd and shepherdess.

Even in Hyde Park the trees had been planted by the same aesthetic eye in linear formations and small clusters. This was the third occasion in as many days since she had been here that Annabel had come here to walk and take the air with Helena. In advance of the so-called "fashionable hour" they had the park nearly to themselves.

"How are you finding England so far?" she asked Helena.

"It is different from Poland in some ways," Helena replied after a pause. "What we eat, for example. And society seems much more...polite I think the word is."

"Yes, society is very polite." Annabel smiled. She thought about the first invitation card she had received only that morning with her name on it. It had been enclosed alongside an identical card to the Roseleys. But it was a sign that her arrival had been noted by society, perhaps after the small dinner party they had given last night to which the Roseleys had invited a dozen of their closest acquaintances to be introduced to her.

"Are the English bound as much by what they

cannot do as by what they can?"

"On some levels."

"I have observed it even in the servants' quarters. One of the undermaids is too terrified to use her common sense without express permission from her superiors."

"And yet this country would not have forged ahead with innovation, industrialization and empire were the national soul truly shackled."

"A paradox then," Helena mused.

They walked past the Serpentine lake. Had she been bound by thinking that, as a woman, she could not declare her feelings to a man? Perhaps she should have been bolder with Henry? Annabel tried to distract herself away from her thoughts by observing the different water fowl. It was too late now in any case.

"You had a visitor call while you were out," Lady Roseley said on their return.

"Oh?" Annabel felt her heart thud against her chest. Had Henry called? She didn't even know where he was or if he and Marek were even still in London.

"A lady called Mrs. Adams."

Annabel swallowed her disappointment.

"I am afraid I had left instructions that I was not at home and so I did not see Mrs. Adams; but she left her card," Lady Roseley continued. "Is she an old friend of yours?"

"I do not recall a Mrs. Adams." Annabel forced herself to smile. Where was Henry? He had been so distant with her on the whole journey. Helena had spent more time with his valet than she had with Henry. Even so, she had not expected him to cut her so completely when they got here.

"I expect that she is an old friend of yours who has since married," Lady Roseley said kindly. "Perhaps you should call on Mrs. Adams tomorrow?"

"Mrs. Adams, eh?" Lord Roseley shut the library door and strode up the hallway towards them.

"Yes, that's right," his wife replied. "Mrs. Thomas Adams."

"Ah. That young man's sister. Well, there's a thing."

"What young man, my dear?" Lady Roseley asked.

"The devil take it!" Roseley growled. "I can't put my finger on his name. Annabel?"

Annabel shrugged her shoulders. There were dozens and dozens of families in London, the so-called *ton*, all seemingly known to one another. But she had forgotten now who exactly was related to whom. It was going to take her a while to learn it all again.

"You know, Annabel, the one who brought you here."

"Mr. Champion?" Annabel shook her head. "That can't be right. He never mentioned a sister."

"Well, he told me all right and dandy that his brother-in-law was a Member of Parliament by the name of Adams, so that makes his sister Mrs. Adams. I know you all think me an old fool but I knew there was something funny going on when he made a fuss about the money."

"What money?" Annabel asked.

"Why don't we go into the drawing room and have some tea?" her aunt suggested.

Annabel felt her arm on her shoulder; it made her realize she trembled. Henry had never said he had a sister. He had said his father was a Naturalist but she could not recall his ever saying anything else about the rest of his family. What else had he not told her?

"You don't think I am going to get a fellow to bring you all the way here from Poland and then not even offer to pay him something for his time and trouble?" Roseley cocked his head. "Anyhow, you can rest easy he is a bona fide gentleman. He absolutely refused to take it. I had to insist, and then he only took it because he wants to buy back his inheritance."

"You *paid* Mr. Champion to bring me home to England?"

"Of course," Roseley said, nodding.

Annabel's stomach lurched.

Chapter Nineteen

Annabel watched the way the light filtered through the lace fringes of her aunt's curtains and cast a pattern of flecks which danced upon the carpet as the curtains moved backwards and forwards in the draft. They had paid Henry to bring her to England.

"Shall we go into the drawing room?" her aunt asked again. "Are you troubled, my dear, you look a little vexed?"

Annabel wanted to cry out with frustration. Instead she bent and kissed her aunt on the cheek. "I am very happy to be home and very grateful that you made it possible for me to travel home so safely."

"Let's take tea." Lady Roseley smiled.

"Shall we take tea a little later?" Annabel wanted to do something, not sit around drinking tea. "I must go and get changed and then I should like to pay a call on Mrs. Adams. Uncle, may I take the carriage?"

No wonder Henry had seemed so detached, so distant, Annabel thought as she climbed the stairs. It was not a huge inconvenience as he and Marck intended on coming to London anyway, but she supposed her presence would have drawn a halt to any amusing diversions that young gentlemen might otherwise get up to on their travels.

No wonder Henry had seemed so impatient to have done with his chore of having to deliver her safely to her relatives. So resentful. His mood had noticeably lightened once they had crossed the channel and only had Kent to travel through before reaching London. He must have been thinking of his own family, his sister, whom he would not have seen for some time.

Annabel walked along the first floor hallway and up the staircase to the second floor and to her room. How foolish she had been to think that he had wanted to rescue her and that Henry had accepted Zakonski's challenge at least in part because he was concerned for her honor. She must learn that her imagination ran riot if she let it. He had only done what he'd done because he was being paid for it.

And yet his sister had called on her and she could not resist the opportunity to meet his sister. Perhaps even, if she went to Mrs. Adams' house, she might see Henry there.

She had a bedchamber and a separate room next door for a dressing room where she found Helena tidying her clothes.

"I need to change out of this carriage dress and into something more suitable for visiting."

"How about the apricot colored one?'"

"I was thinking perhaps the gray serge?"

"No." Helena pursued her lips. "Too old and unbecoming. You should give that dress away to a charitable institution. Why you even bothered to pack it and bring it with you I don't know."

"I will wear my gray dress."

"No you won't. Dismiss me if you like but I won't help you put it on. Indeed I will rip it to shreds before you put it on." Helena's expression was fierce. "You know I am just protecting your best interests."

"Helena, I am not visiting a man. In fact, if you must know, I am going to visit Mrs. Adams who is Mr. Champion's sister."

"And you think men look at clothes? Ha! If it is a lady you are seeing then all the more reason to take care. What will she think of you if you turn up in that old rag?"

"That I am an honorable matron of good standing I hope."

"I do not work for a matron. I work for Countess Szalynski whose dress sense is impeccable. What about the moss-green one? With the sable trimmed pelisse?"

"I concede." Annabel knew Helena was right and would listen. She didn't begrudge Helena having her say. The gray was hideous. And it was pleasant to have someone who cared enough to speak out. "I will wear the green one."

Annabel waited as Helena undid the buttons down her back.

"I hope you will forgive my impertinence in advising you not to wear the gray," Helena said. "I am not an English servant, you see, or I would never have said such a thing."

"Of course." Annabel hardly heard her for she was lost in her own reverie. Henry had once told her he found her fascinating. He had kissed her. He had danced with her. And he had lain with her in her bed that evening at her behest, cradling her in his arms. He'd wanted to make love to her until she had pushed him away.

She helped Helena by removing her arms from their sleeves and stepping out of the dress while Helena held it to the floor. Annabel knew she wanted to put her head in her hands and cry but that would achieve nothing. Henry had her heart. He must either take her on as well, or she wanted her heart back for herself.

Helena put away her dress and carefully brought out the green one.

"Helena, have you ever been in love?" she found herself asking suddenly.

Helena turned around and to Annabel's great surprise was blushing. "Indeed, I fear I may be," she said.

"Oh, I am sorry. I did not intend to pry into your private feelings."

"No, I am happy to speak of it." Helena turned back towards the chest. "You may be less surprised to hear that the man in question is Mr. Champion's valet. Now, Robards has a very fine eye for detail in dress and you must look perfect." She smiled. "And so must I, for I assume I am to accompany you to Mrs. Adams' house? Hopefully Mr. Champion and his valet are there as well."

Helena was exactly right. She must look her very best and go and see his sister. This was no time to be timid. At the very least, if Henry wasn't there, she should be able to find out where he was and what he was doing. At best she might become acquainted with the sister and have the possibility of seeing Henry again. She wondered if Helena and Robards had been in communication with one another since they had arrived in London.

****

An hour later, Annabel looked up at the square, double-fronted house. A building of similar size and stature to its neighbors, it sat on a quiet road off the main street which ran through the village of Highgate. *Was* Henry here?

Helena was led away presumably to partake of some refreshment in the servants' quarters and the butler showed Annabel into a large drawing room pleasantly furnished in a fashionable style. She waited alone for some minutes and passed the time looking at the collection of ornaments displayed on the shelves of a rosewood whatnot.

Mrs. Adams burst in like a whirlwind. Oh, how like Henry she was! Blonde hair, the same nose, the same mouth, a similar smile. Annabel could tell at once she could be no other than Henry's sister.

"Countess Szalynski, how so very good of you to call," she said. "You will take tea will you not? I have already rung for it in any case." Mrs. Adams swept her skirts away in a sudden motion of her hand and seated herself on the chaise next to her.

"I am delighted to meet you and so pleased that you called," Annabel replied. The other woman's warmth was contagious.

"Oh, it was the least I could do. I have to confess I was curious to meet you. Henry has been, well, so difficult since he came home. He wants to see you, I know; but he is making such a complete ham of it I thought I would take the matter into my own hands. There, I have made my confession and our tea has not yet even arrived!" Mrs. Adams leaned forward and spoke in a softer voice. "I do hope you will forgive me."

"I had no idea until you called that Henry had a sister. He..." Annabel was unsure what she meant or wanted to say. She bit her tongue. "Had I known, I should have already called on you."

"One must never leave the machinations of social discourse to gentlemen!" Mrs. Adams exclaimed. "They think only of themselves and who they might play at cards at their club in the evening. As to the rest of society it could pass them by in the blink of an eyelid. Give a man a purpose and he will achieve it. Ask him to juggle the balls of dozens of acquaintances for years upon years with no determinate goal and... Well, he will leave the balls on the floor and go to his club!"

"Oh!" Annabel could not remember when she had laughed so much. "My late husband was just the same. If it was political or a hunting party he was interested. If not, I might not see him for days!"

"Days? Ha! I have not seen my brother for years at a time, so intent he has been on his wanderings. But he tells me he is to stay in England now. He's staying with us at present. He wants to go into the House of Commons, become a Member of

Parliament. In fact he has gone up to town today with my husband to see someone about it."

Annabel tried not to dwell on her disappointment. Henry was not here now, but at least she knew that he was staying with his sister and had not yet gone to Leicestershire.

"He told me about his ambitions in Poland," she said to Mrs. Adams. "Do you not think it will suit him? He told me that he wanted English children to be able to play in fields like the Polish children, not shut in factories working. He was so sincere in his convictions, I wanted to cry—" She could not help herself any longer. Real tears came. She blinked them back but could not prevent one sliding down her cheek.

"Oh, you poor thing!" Mrs. Adams' arms were around her in a moment. "Henry has been thoughtless, I know. But we shall win him around."

Annabel felt quite embarrassed and fumbled in her reticule for her handkerchief.

Mrs. Adams moved back to her chaise.

"I am sorry," Annabel started. "I have only just met you and—"

"Shush! Listen to me." Mrs. Adams leaned forward and took Annabel's hand. "It is what he wants too but, well, things have been difficult. Henry didn't have an ordinary childhood. Our father was quite obsessed with his work. He never gave Henry the attention he needed and our mother tried to make up for it. But when it came down to it, she always put our father first. They sent Henry away to school when he was very young."

"He told me this—"

"But did he tell you that we ended up on a plantation in Barbados?"

Annabel shook her head.

"We were guests of the plantation owner, courtesy of some favor he owed to some aristocratic friend back in England. Quite how our father managed to get support for his travels I do not know; but I know that he dedicated his works to his patrons and these included members of some of the leading families in the land. I think the plantation owner was kind enough to us as it goes, but we saw some shocking things. Things that they did to the slaves that you could hardly imagine. Henry hated it all. He was only a small child but he saw and felt the cruelty in ways that perhaps the rest of us did not. Eventually, we came back to England, and shortly after our parents both died of the Scarlet Fever. I expect he told you this?"

Annabel nodded.

"You see he finds it so difficult to express his emotions."

"He had been quite short with me during our journey from Krakow," Annabel admitted.

Mrs. Adams sat back in the chair, a fixed and serious expression on her face. "I know he loves you, loves you very much." Her voice remained soft. "He has been black as thunder since he's been home. Even his friend Count Ralenski has been on him."

Annabel felt her tears prick all the harder. She pulled her handkerchief across her face, breathed in and tried to sit up straight.

"What are your plans now you are in England?" Mrs. Adams asked.

"I am staying as you know with Lord and Lady Roseley who are my uncle and aunt. We are in London for a week or two and then I think we go to their estate in Yorkshire for the summer."

"For the whole summer?"

"Yes, I expect so."

"Oh, dear. I don't think Henry has any reason to be in Yorkshire. Perhaps you might come here for a longer visit. A day or two? If I invite you, will you come?"

"Yes, that would be very kind." Annabel ventured a smile.

"Splendid, then I shall have a house party and that way I am sure that you will manage to talk to Henry alone. You must remember the old saying. It is, you can lead a horse to water but you cannot make it drink."

Annabel nodded. She saw at once the horse was Henry.

"We must make sure that the water is not so far away as Yorkshire when the horse realizes that he is thirsty!"

****

"Henry, I have met Countess Szalynski," Jane said at dinner that evening, utterly confounding him. "She called today and she is charming."

"She called? Here…?"

"The Countess," Marek said, bowing his head slightly, "is a delightful lady."

Henry wanted to hit Marek. Hard. As for his interfering sister—

"If you insist on bringing a lady to London from the other side of Europe the least you can do is marry her," his brother-in-law said.

"Is it quite the thing, do you think, to discuss a lady who is absent and almost completely unknown to you at dinner?" Henry asked.

"Touché," Thomas replied, smiling.

"Family dinners! It is always the same," Marek said.

"You know, Henry, I have been thinking. You are going up to Sevenoaks soon, aren't you?" Jane smiled at him and Henry was grateful his sister had been so kind as to change the subject.

"Yes, of course. In fact, if Count Ralenski is agreeable, I thought we might pop up there next week."

"I am certainly agreeable."

"Good," Jane continued. "As you will be here for another week I think we will hold a small house party. I trust you are agreeable and will not vex me by disappearing at the eleventh hour?"

"Of course not," Henry conceded, though he was sure that his sister was up to something.

"There are a number of our acquaintances we must ask," Jane said. "And some people whom the count should meet."

"If they are female and pretty, I should be delighted to make their acquaintance, madam,'" Marek answered.

"And what about your acquaintances, Henry? And the officers from your old regiment?"

"I shall leave the guest list entirely in your hands, sister." Henry expected that this was what she wanted to hear. "But this is a house party? Not a grand entertainment?"

"And we must ask Countess Szalynski," Jane added.

Henry spluttered on his soup. He dropped his spoon. "Of course." He kept his tone entirely even and retrieved the spoon slowly. He hoped no one had noticed.

"Splendid!" Jane exclaimed. "I shall arrange it all without delay."

From the way his sister smiled he knew that was it. Her plan was that she would hold a house party and that the countess would simply fall at his feet. Her simplicity of mind was charming but Jane didn't know Annabel at all. She would never marry him because he was far too ordinary for her. She had been the Honorable Miss Annabel Wells, and was now a countess whereas he was just a two-a-penny English gentleman. However, he could not deny that he was looking forward to the prospect of seeing her again.

****

Henry looked up from his newspaper to see Jane standing above him with a piece of note paper in one hand and a pencil in the other.

"I have just come to talk to you about the house party," she said. "We have had several more acceptances today. They are all on the desk I am using in the Morning Room if you want to peruse them yourself."

"What Henry really wants to know is, has Countess Szalynski accepted her invitation yet?" Marek said.

It was, in truth, the question Henry wanted to ask. He decided that hearing the answer was more important than deciding whether he should take Marek outside and wring his neck. So much for a peaceful hour trying to get himself up to speed on the issues of the day by reading the paper.

"Countess Szalynski?" Jane looked a picture of innocence. "Why, yes. I had a note from her today."

"And? What was her answer? Tell me!" Henry held his breath.

"Why, she is coming. Of course I had mentioned the party to her when we met, so I had hoped that she would attend. It will be pleasant for Count Ralenski to have a familiar face here, don't you think, Henry?"

Henry did not deign to answer and stalked off to walk around the gardens. He had a good idea that his sister was teasing him.

****

Not many days later Henry sat in the drawing room feeling languid although his mind still raced. A light breeze from the garden came in through the open French doors and brushed his face. Opposite him sat Marek and Thomas, his brother-in-law, both of whom appeared to be half-asleep. On the far sofa sat Jane and his brother-in-law's unmarried sister Belinda who had just arrived from Essex. Belinda appeared to have a lively manner and she conversed at great speed with Jane.

"Everybody is coming. I don't know quite what we are going to do with them all," Jane said. She sat with note paper on her lap and a slight frown on her face. "Now, do you think I should order five hundred extra candles from the chandler? Will that be enough?"

"Perhaps seven hundred," Belinda suggested, "to be sure not to run out."

"Five thousand," Henry said.

"Five thousand candles, Henry? Isn't that just a little extravagant?"

"Yes, precisely. And I was wondering about those Chinese lanterns. Can we get several hundred of those, to illuminate the terraces and the gardens? Can we get some fellow to build a pagoda on the lawn?"

"Pagoda on the lawn?" Jane's frown deepened. "I don't think—"

"Only for the evening. There was one, Marek, you remember don't you? That Russian count who had more money than he knew what to do with and who held a garden party in Vienna in the middle of the snow. He had a whole Chinese landscape built for it and it was all heated with some kind of hot air system. Very clever. I didn't shiver once during the whole night."

"Perhaps with some simple woodwork and bales of calico we can make some kind of tent? Is that what you mean, Henry?"

"Yes, yes, but it has to look authentic."

"How am I supposed to know what an authentic Chinese pagoda looks like? Henry, you do realize the house party is next week?"

"Dear lady, come over here." Marek got up from his chair and went over to a display cabinet where he pointed at one of the porcelain plates. Jane followed him. "See, a pagoda with a roof just like a little hat, and a little bridge leading up to it, surrounded by Willow trees."

Henry leapt to his feet and came over to see the plate. "That's it! The very scene. We will need an ornamental bridge and I know just the place for it. Leading from the third terrace it could take the guests over that rather useless flowerbed and right into the middle of the main lawn."

"Thank you, Count Ralenski." Jane gave him a smile and Henry a glare. "*You* are most helpful."

"And firecrackers!" Henry said, ignoring her. Making the party fantastic was far more important. He would show Annabel that he was no ordinary English gentleman. Not even the Russian had had fireworks at his party. He smiled.

Chapter Twenty

They went riding that afternoon. After a brisk canter across meadows they had to pass through some woodland on a track. Henry, deep in thought about exactly how the scene would unfold when Annabel arrived in Highgate, found himself dawdling behind.

"Miss Adams, you handle a horse like a Polishwoman!" Marek, who trotted in front of him at Belinda's side, said.

Henry felt his eyebrows lift. This was high praise indeed. Marek was generally scornful about women who claimed to be able to ride well turning out to be frauds.

"That is because I was brought up in the saddle," Belinda replied.

"My dear lady, how is it that you are not married and have a clutch of sparkly-eyed children hanging from your skirts?"

"I have not yet found a gentleman to suit."

"Ah! What about a Polish gentleman?"

Henry stiffened. Marek's flirtation appeared to be going a bit far. Should he step in? Belinda had no chaperone present. Both Jane and Thomas were a little way ahead of them, well out of earshot.

"I had not considered whether a Polish gentleman would suit," Belinda replied.

Henry pulled back a bit. Belinda had been out in society for at least two or three years and was most likely perfectly capable of handling a mild flirtation.

"How about if the Polish gentleman was a count of good family and fortune and an ex-hussar?"

Was this more than flirtation? Was Marek being serious? His words were tantamount to a proposal of marriage.

"Oh! How dashing!"

"A gentleman who had traveled Europe and met hundreds and hundreds of ladies and yet never fallen in love with any of them?"

No, Henry thought Marek was not being serious. He was teasing.

"I should think him feckless!" Belinda said.

"Feckless, not...discerning?" Marek asked.

"That would depend on the gentleman."

"What about that Count Ralenski fellow?"

Bells and whistles! Marek was serious?

"He might suit," Belinda said as if she talked about a dress she was considering having made.

Henry flicked the reins of his mount, and in a moment caught up with them. When had this sudden romance started blossoming and why had he been so blind as not to see it? "What do you say to a race down the hill and to home?" he suggested.

Henry drew Marek to one side after they had dismounted and walked on their way back to the house from the stables.

"Marek, I realize you are a somewhat accomplished gallant, but I feel I must come down on you a bit heavily for your remarks to Miss Adams earlier. They, well, I think you were close to stepping over the line."

"Henry, I will not discuss a lady with you, even one related to you by marriage. What happens between us is our own affair until such a time as it is right for me to approach her father."

"Are you telling me your intentions toward Miss Adams are serious?"

"I am telling you, since you clearly wish to be told something, to go and find the romance in your own soul. Here." Marek stooped down and pointed at a daisy growing in a tuft of grass next to the path. "See this flower? Imagine this flower is the woman you are in love with."

"Marek, what—"

"Now if I talk to this little flower, nurture it, keep it watered and in the sunlight, it will look as pretty for me as it does today."

"This is nonsense."

"Is it? Now listen." Marek nipped the flower at its stem and stood up. He held it up in front of him. "Suppose I throw the flower over there, on those flagstones?" He did just that. "Now I leave it there, ignore it. Soon it will begin to wither away. And eventually, dust."

"Thank you. I see exactly what you are saying. What do you think the damn house party is for?"

"Ah, but can you afford to wait that long?"

Henry turned his head away and quickened his pace. He was not listening to any more of this. What was it with being back in England that suddenly gave everyone the right to order him around? No wonder he'd preferred it when his decisions were all his own.

****

Later Henry spied Belinda lying on the chaise in the conservatory reading a copy of *The Ladies Magazine*. He retreated before she saw him. He didn't know where Marek was but the house seemed very quiet. He padded through the downstairs hallway towards the Morning Room.

Can you afford to wait that long? Marek had said. Henry had not seen or had any personal contact with Annabel since they had arrived back in England three weeks ago.

He paused outside the Morning Room door, listened out of habit before realizing that it was nonsense that he should be creeping around like this.

Henry looked around the door, happy the room was empty. He spotted at once two tall piles of letters on the left-hand side of the small escritoire that must be the house party replies.

He would write Annabel a letter but he was disinclined for the fact to become public knowledge.

It would only be a brief letter saying how he was delighted that she'd had time to make the acquaintance of his sister in London, how he hoped she was enjoying England and that he looked forward to seeing her. He hoped she was still in London, for as long as he posted it by tomorrow morning she would receive it the next day. There would be plenty of time for her to pen a reply if it suited her.

Annabel's reply was on the top of the second pile. Henry picked it up. He found himself thinking of the feel of the thick paper in his fingers; this very paper would have been touched by her hands. He liked the look of her writing, bold yet feminine. He read:

Countess Szalynski would be delighted to attend the house party to be held on 29th June and thanks Mrs. Thomas Adams for her kind invitation.

He cast the paper back on the top of the pile. He was about to turn on his heel when he realized the paper just below it had caught his eye. He pulled it out. The very same paper. A reply from Lord and Lady Roseley.

So Jane had also invited the Roseleys! Why, in heaven's name did she have to interfere? Why couldn't she just leave it alone! He stuffed the Roseley's reply back into the pile and wanted at that moment to pick up the whole damn lot and throw them on the fire.

Except that the fire in the Morning Room wasn't

lit today. The weather was too warm.

Henry stalked out of the room, slamming the door behind him.

He'd be damned if he was writing a letter to Annabel at the Roseley's when it was less than an hour's ride away. He would pay a social call tomorrow afternoon and say to her in person the things he would have written about.
****

Belinda laughed at every poor joke which Marek made at breakfast the following morning. Henry bit into his toast, dimly aware that part of what he felt was frustration.

He was taking delivery of two fine geldings this morning so he could not go into town any sooner. According to Jane they were starting work on building the pagoda framework and she wanted him to make sure that he explained to the men the plan he'd drawn up. So he had this morning to work out what he was going to say to Annabel this afternoon. It had seemed simple yesterday, now less so.

He was a man, wasn't he? Not some hideously shy adolescent plucking up the courage for the first time to ask a lady to dance.

And this was Annabel. Annabel who had looked at him with the very depths of her eyes, who had quivered at his touch, who had responded to his kiss.

Why, why did he feel so damnably frightened?

Because he could not bear the thought that she might reject him once again.
****

The Roseley's London house had been built at the time of Queen Anne and of red brick. It stood on a wide street just off Berkeley Square.

Henry's geldings had arrived and the pagoda was being constructed to his plan. Now for his third, and most significant task of the day. He rapped on the large, black front door.

"Not at home," the butler said after opening the door.

"What do you mean, not at home?"

The butler looked at him curiously and shook his head.

"I'm sorry if I am a little off the mark on matters of precise etiquette," Henry said. "I am a...close friend of the family. This is rather urgent. Could you please tell me when you expect Countess Szalynski to be at home? Or Lady Roseley?"

"Not expected back until tomorrow, or the day after, sir."

This was no good, no good at all. "Where have they gone?"

"Lester Park, sir," the butler answered.

Lester Park was Jonathan Harvey's family home. In Surrey.

"Thank you." Henry turned and walked down the few steps and back onto the pavement where the cab still waited. "From which public house can I get a coach to Surrey?" he asked the jarvey. There was no time to go back to Highgate and borrow a carriage. He was going to have to find some public transport if he was to get to Lester Park today. His old friend Jonathan was going to have an unexpected guest.

****

Henry wasn't prepared for the sight that hit him, a tableau of domesticity which he took in with his eyes but otherwise played no part. It might have been a painting, entitled *An English Summer's Day*; a painting that showed the movement of the actors, the sunshine, the light breeze.

His throat tickled. He wanted to cough, clear it. He daren't. Not yet. They would see him.

Lady Roseley and another lady sat with their backs to him at the top of the lawn under a large parasol.

To their left, in the middle of the lawn was a wicket. In front of it stood a small boy wielding a cricket bat. Behind him crouched Jonathan Harvey to catch any stray balls. To their left stood another small boy staring at the batsman with remarkable concentration as a fielder. He seemed under instruction from Lord Roseley who stood beside him.

Skipping forward to bowl the next ball was Annabel. She wore a light white dress that moved against her legs in the breeze.

Henry stared. She bowled underarm a straight ball. The boy missed and Jonathan caught the slow moving ball easily.

"Never mind, next one," Jonathan called. He threw it back to Annabel.

She caught it, easily and gracefully. Henry realized he wanted to scoop her up into his arms at that very moment. He wanted to carry her off somewhere.

The small batsman looked up and saw him. "Are you coming to play, sir?" he said.

They all turned and stared at Henry, standing there watching but not involved in the game. He ran his fingers through his hair and stepped down onto the lawn.

"What a marvelous cricket bat," he said to the boy.

"Uncle Jonathan gave it to me," came the enthusiastic reply.

So it was Uncle Jonathan was it? These must be his sister's children. Just like he was uncle to his own sister's children, Caroline and little Thomas. Henry felt a pang of regret. He'd never played cricket with them. He would buy Thomas a marvelous bat as soon as he was old enough.

"Henry." Annabel hurried towards him. Even as she rushed she seemed to have a grace about her that he'd somehow not noticed before.

"Are you going to play with us?" the boy persisted. "It's my birthday today."

"Happy birthday." Henry ruffled the boy's hair.

"Come on, young scamp." Jonathan walked over. "Back to the game." He looked at Henry. "Henry, how good to see you. Although I don't exactly believe I invited you here today. Is something wrong?"

"No, nothing is wrong. Actually, old chap, I've come to see A— Countess Szalynski." Henry shrugged his shoulders. "A brief word, that's all. I won't keep her away from you for long."

"Go ahead, Henry. We're stopping for tea soon in any case. You're welcome to join us."

"Henry." Annabel reached him. "How are you? What a surprise to see you."

"So you are not going to play with us?" Jonathan's nephew puffed his chest out and stood tall.

Henry placed his hands on the knees of his breeches and crouched down, looked the young upstart in the eye and said, "Not today. I have actually come today to see the countess. You don't mind, do you? I am afraid I did not know that it was your birthday; but next time I come I'll bring you your present."

He watched the conflicting emotions play across the child's face. He wondered what he would have made of it all as a seven or eight-year-old being asked to make a very adult decision and act with adult generosity.

"You may," the boy said at last. "Don't forget about the present."

"I won't. Gentleman's honor," Henry replied, rising.

"You came to see me?" Annabel said, her brows knotted slightly and her voice not much louder than a whisper. She stood just a foot away from him. The breeze blew a tendril of her hair across her face and she raised her hand and pushed it away.

"You don't think I'd bother to come all this way just to see my old friend Mr. Harvey, do you?" Henry replied. "Can you be let out of the game so you can accompany me for a turn about the gardens?"

"Certainly." Annabel smiled.

Henry told himself to remember to breathe and offered her his arm.

He raised his hat and waved it at Lady Roseley and the unknown lady who might be Jonathan's sister. They were all watching, he knew, as surely as if their stares were actually boring into his back as Annabel and he walked. They strolled to the base of the lawn and then alongside the lake, side by side.

Her steps matched his perfectly. He had no need to hurry or slow down. He ambled, holding his hands behind his back, towards the copse to the right of the lake, the woodland path and privacy.

"Have you been enjoying your time in England?"

Annabel turned her head towards him so that she saw his face, the line of his nose, framed by the lake and landscape behind him. She didn't at first know how to answer. She'd been miserable at the start, sinking lower and lower as she'd had no word from him. She'd been buoyed by meeting his sister, and then flattened again when she had heard nothing from him directly. And now here he was and she was elated.

"Some things have been a little difficult," she said, "like trying to remember exactly who is related to whom; but I am enjoying myself now." *Because you are here*, she thought but dared not say. "How is Marek?"

"There is a strong possibility," Henry said, his gaze fixed on the path ahead, "that Marek is in love."

"Truly?" The prospect of that event was delightful. "Can I ask who the lady is?"

"My brother-in-law's sister, Belinda, who is

staying with us at present. I think Marek is serious because he won't talk about it and turns my enquiries against me, making up fables about flowers and the like."

"How wonderful!" Annabel said. "I only hope, and Henry I am only saying this to you because you know Marek so well, that she will lick him into shape."

"He is already eating out of her hand."

"Ah, then it must be love." There was a skip to her step and she saw, perhaps properly for the first time, how gentle the English sunshine was as it filtered through the swaying leaves of the trees and cast moving patterns on the grass below.

"You know who else is in love?" Annabel said.

"No. Who?"

The man beside her progressed forward too absolutely to be affected by the sunshine or the breeze. Annabel wondered if she dared lay her hand on his arm. She wanted to. That they would see her do so from the lawn above she did not care about.

"Helena, my maid; and guess who the lucky man is?"

"How can I guess?"

"You know him very well, I think. In fact you see him every day."

"Don't tell me she has fallen for Marek too!"

"No!" Annabel laughed. "Your man, Robards."

"Ah, yes, I did wonder for he did let one or two things slip. Well, well, we shall have to make sure they have the opportunity to spend some time together." Henry's voice sounded very light. As he spoke she began to imagine he was talking about their future, as much as Helena and Robards.

"This way." Henry stopped and turned to the left as the path came to a fork. He offered her his arm with a nod. She took it, a sparkling something suddenly filling her from the tips of her toes to the top of her head. He swept her onwards, towards and then into a small woodland.

The air felt cooler. They were out of the sun— but not cold. The trees rustled. A small pitch-black colored bird with a bright orange beak hopped out of their way.

"Oh, we have those birds in Poland, Henry. Did you see? The black one. What are they called again? I am so hopeless, you'd never think I grew up in England."

"That's a blackbird."

"A blackbird! Of course." Annabel giggled. "How could I have forgotten."

Henry shook his shoulders as a sudden gust ruffled the hair at the back of his neck. Or was it her? Did his skin prickle just because she stood beside him, her hand resting on his arm?

He had stopped and so had she.

"Annabel," he began. Then he thought that at this moment with her gazing up into his eyes, waiting, trusting, he didn't really want to speak to her. Words were not, could never be, enough.

His hands felt their way to drawing her head towards him; his bare fingers teased the sides of her hair. He bent down, pulled her against him, into his crushing warmth, towards the inevitable.

His lips fell on hers.

Soft and pliant she yielded to the touch.

He'd tasted her before, thought he knew, and he pushed the gentle brush of lips upon lips into a harder, more demanding kiss. He was unprepared for the jolt that coursed through him as she met his force with her own. Henry wound his arms around her back and held her even tighter. He wanted to make her part of him, to warrant his mastery.

Still she teased him, her tongue entwining around his and touching his teeth. Did she realize what flames she stoked? He delved deeper, forgetting where he was. He explored. Savored. Took.

He found it a supreme effort of will to pull back, to end the kiss he never wanted to end. She stumbled backwards and so he let himself continue to hold her. He tried to overcome the pulsing ache in his head, the unwanted tightness of his breeches, the racing of his heart.

He found his way to looking into her eyes. Eyes that danced, though they were wide with shock, perhaps desire. His blood pounded all the more. How had it happened that everything he wanted was in this one woman who stood before him? That his entire happiness should rest on one small set of shoulders?

"Annabel," he heard himself say, "will you marry me?"

Chapter Twenty-One

Henry felt faint.

"... me to marry you?"

He shook himself. He'd been so busy despising himself for such womanish inclinations he'd only caught the very end of what she said.

"Sorry?" He wished most vehemently he was less of a fool.

"Henry, why do you wish for me to marry you?"

What sort of devil of a question was that? He was a fool. Did she think this was easy? She was supposed to fall at his feet about now, not start interrogating him like the Spanish Inquisition.

"I am not sure what you mean." He tried to keep his tone from sounding gruff. "I want to marry you so that you will be my wife. It is simple. Isn't it?"

The way she looked at him made him not so sure.

"I hadn't planned on asking you for your hand today as it happens," he said. "I was going to ask you at my sister's house party. But then I realized I did not want to wait." He drew one hand away from her so that he could pull at his now ticklish cravat.

"On top of that you provoked me into it even earlier. With that kiss."

"You kissed me," she said, far too evenly for his liking.

"Anyhow, I've messed up it appears by forgetting all the pretty speeches I am supposed to give in advance of the final question. I wanted to praise your beauty and accomplishments. Well, you are beautiful, Annabel, very beautiful, but you know that already. And accomplished, of course. All those languages you speak so fluently for a start. If I carry on, can I make it up to you? I was going to have a speech prepared. I was even considering whether I could manage verse. Nothing too complicated, just rhyming couplets…"

Henry stilled. A tear was gliding down her left cheek. He raised his finger, caught it and brushed it away. He didn't know what else he could do.

Then she started crying. Oh, he really was making a mull of everything.

"Annabel, what would you like me to do? Shall I try a pretty speech? It might not be very good. Do you want a handkerchief?" He pulled out his handkerchief in any case and gave it to her.

"Shall I kiss you again?" he suggested.

"No, thank you, Henry. Can you take me back to the house?"

Bells and whistles! He had completely and utterly blown it. What could he do? He tried to force his mind to race but it wouldn't. It was sticky as treacle. He couldn't think; he just had to let go of her and offer her his arm.

"I'm sorry, Annabel, for being such a fool. It is probably the worst proposal you've ever received. Tell me what to do and I'll make it up to you. Is there a chance you will listen to me if I speak to you at the house party? As I had planned?"

She took his arm but her eyes remained cast to the ground. Damnation! What if she wouldn't even grant him a second go?

"Oh, Annabel, it's just that I love you so much. It's so frightfully confusing. You don't know what it was like all those years ago. I thought that was bad, but now, now it is a hundred times worse. You don't know how terrified I am that I'll lose you."

"You…you love me?" She halted, looked up and blinked her tears away.

"Yes." Henry replied, breathless. He could really do with having a tree or something to lean against. She was all right, she could lean on him.

"I love you." She placed her hand in his. He clasped it tight. "I think I did then, ten years ago, or at least a little bit. But I was so young and I didn't understand what I was really doing."

"Then why on earth won't you marry me now?" he demanded. He knew now why older men had heart attacks when faced with such a merry-go-round of emotion. It was enough to tempt the patience of a saint. He wanted a damned good reason from her or he wasn't letting her go back to the house and out of his life. Nothing would move him to—

"I am afraid." She lowered her gaze to the ground. He gently lifted her chin so their gazes locked again.

"Afraid? What of?"

"Of part of what it is to be a wife," she whispered, biting her lip.

"Do you mean?" He wasn't sure, but was this to do with why she had pushed him away that night at the castle. "But you've been a wife before? Did he—?"

"No, no." She shook her head. "Nothing like that. Szalynski was a good and gentle man in that regard, but we did not... We did not share a bed." She faltered. Another tear slid down her cheek.

"Please explain," Henry coaxed. "If you can."

"I did not want children. I expect you consider that a little unnatural?"

"Yes. Tell me why you thought as you did, and whether you still think in this way. I confess I had given the matter very little thought until I met you again in Poland. But when I saw you on horseback I also had a vision of our children and how they would take after you in being brave and noble."

"I am not brave." She shook her head.

231

"You truly do not wish to have children?"

"I wish to have your children, Henry, but I cannot—"

"Why not?"

"Because I am afraid to die. My mother died having me. I killed her. And my father too, for he shot himself with the grief of it."

Henry kicked the stump of a tree conveniently close to his foot. He could take her into his arms now, stroke her hair and say *there, there.* But these were feelings of hers that ran deep, feelings that she had perhaps not spoken to many people about, if any.

"Nonsense!" he said. The only way she'd deal with her fears would be if she could be made to face up to them. "There is always a risk in childbed. But tell me, did your grandmother die in childbed too?"

"No. She had a riding accident."

"Or her mother, your great-grandmother?"

"No. She lived to a very good age, until she was in her nineties."

"Or any other of your female relatives."

"No."

"It hardly runs in your blood then, does it?"

"I had never thought about it like that."

"Do you not see that it is a random act? Like my parents catching the Scarlet Fever. We cannot control everything that happens in our lives."

"No. I know that now."

She looked so miserable he forced a smile onto his face. "Some things we can control, dear Annabel. Sometimes happiness is there if we are willing to take a chance on it."

"Yes," she said. Her eyes sparkled like the sunshine on the lake. "I will marry you, Henry. I will."

A word about the author...

Kate Allan lives in Bedfordshire, England, in the countryside close to the Chiltern Hills, with her husband, son and West Highland White Terrier.

Krakow Waltz is her fifth Regency romance. She is the author of *Fateful Deception*, shortlisted for the Romantic Novelists' Association Joan Hessayson New Writers' Award, and co-author, with Michelle Styles, of *The Lady Soldier* by Jennifer Lindsay.

Her website: www.kateallan.com